INSINCERITY

by
Richard Godwin

This paperback edition published in Great Britain in 2018 by
Black Jackal Books, Suite 106, 143 Kingston Road,
London SW19 1LJ

ISBN: 978-0-9567113-7-3

Book layout by Guido Henkel
Cover design by Lieu Pham, Covertopia.com

Papers used by Black Jackal Books are natural renewable and
recyclable products sourced from well-managed forests and
certified in accordance with the rules of the Forest Stewardship
Council.

Printed by ImprintDigital.com, Exeter, United Kingdom

For Page

1

Friday 10:00 AM.

Tammy Wayne knew the voice, cold, metallic, lacking intonation. It hummed in her head like a tuning fork as she peered through the Venetian blinds of her office in Fulham down into the bright street below. It was an idle gesture. She knew he wouldn't be out there. He was too smart. She said nothing, hoping to hold him long enough to get the trace on the phone call. Waiting for the man who called himself The Pimp to make a mistake.

'I can't hear you, it's a bad line,' she said, keeping her voice steady, controlled.

'I have things to give you, all that frozen skin, piece by broken piece,' he said.

'I'm going to find you and kill you for what you did.'

'I hope you enjoy your sister's mouth.'

2

The first explosion ripped through the outer wall, tearing the facade from the office block. A chair and a desk landed on the pavement, their legs rolling into the traffic as cars swerved to avoid them. The second explosion came exactly two minutes later and removed the entire floor of the building. Two pedestrians were injured by falling debris and it took the fire brigade several hours to put out the fire.

Tammy Wayne had gone out on an unexpected call after The Pimp ended the call. She narrowly missed being there when the building was blown apart. A woman called Joyce Farmer had rung a few minutes before his call, claiming to know The Pimp's identity. Joyce said enough for her to suspect she was not a hoaxer. As it was, the call saved her life.

She drove out of Fulham, to the address in Shepherd's Bush that Joyce had given her. As Tammy stepped out of her immaculate black Mercedes Coupe two young guys whistled. She was used to the attention, looking like a model, blonde and full figured, with deep azure eyes that seemed to fill her face with a piece of the sky. She worked out each day, running and lifting weights and she had muscle, but it didn't clash with her femininity.

Tammy ignored them and bought a ticket from a machine, stuck it on the dashboard of her car and wondered how much hotter it was going to get. It was already in the eighties and it wasn't even noon. The heat didn't help when she was under such intense surveillance. The Pimp watching her every move, she didn't even like to keep her windows open at night. Sunlight blasted off the burning metal of her car, like an exploding flashlight on the baking street. She walked up to the door and pressed the bell.

A few moments later a grey-haired, attractive woman in her sixties opened the door. She had a hint of lipstick on, but otherwise wore no makeup.

'Mrs Farmer?' Tammy said.

'Come in, and please, it's Joyce.'

As Tammy stepped into the hallway the smell of detergent hit her. Joyce took Tammy into a small neat kitchen and made coffee, then took a tray through into the living room. It was tastefully designed, pastel colours and prints in silver frames. The room was spotless, so clean it looked unused. Tammy sat on a chair while Joyce sank into the deep sofa opposite.

'I know the man you're looking for,' Joyce said. 'I've read about you in the newspaper, terrible what he did to your sister, I hear he's taken the lives of eight women.'

'And you're sure you know him?'

'As sure as a woman can be. I guess my profession helped me.'

'Helped you how?'

Joyce held her gaze, then looked away. Tammy sipped the coffee.

'He's a toolmaker, he used to visit me.'

'Visit you for what?' Tammy said.

'Not all hookers work the streets, I called myself an escort but it's the same thing.'

'He was a client?'

Joyce paused. She seemed to be lost in a recollection that Tammy could tell was not of a pleasant nature, her eyes downcast. Tammy looked at her and waited for her to speak. Joyce was good-looking for her age, in good shape, and Tammy wondered if she'd had work done.

'That's right, he was a client,' Joyce said, 'and he was obsessed by mouths. I've read the papers.'

'It's one of the things he collects. Did he ever do anything to you?'

'He had unusual sexual tastes, he liked dominating, which is not surprising.'

'And why do you think he's The Pimp?'

'Because he talked to me about women's lips. The way he spoke about them used to make me want to wash him from my skin, and I had all sorts of creeps visit me.'

'Do you mind if I write this down?' Tammy said, getting out a small blue pocket book and a gold pen.

'Not at all honey.'

'Can you tell me what he said?'

'He'd say, "You can tell from a woman's mouth what kind of whore she is." Those were his words I'm pretty sure.'

'Do you know his name?'

'Tricks don't give hookers their names. But I can tell you what he looked like then, ten years ago when he used to visit me.' Joyce picked a packet of

Dunhills off the glass topped coffee table in front of her, pulled one from the pack, and lit it with a Zippo lighter, narrowing her eyes as she took a drag. Tammy waited, pen poised. 'I'd say he's six foot, not a bad looking man, it may surprise you to hear, not the kind of man who couldn't get a woman if he wanted, confident, assured, but his needs would make most woman afraid. His eyes are strange, almost as if you can see through them, but he's reading you all the time, watchful.'

'You mentioned his sexual needs.'

'He never did anything to me, but he once showed me a knife he'd made, that's how I know his profession, you see. It was a steel handled serrated knife, long, sharp as a razor. He stood there holding it out in front of me and I was scared. I could tell that aroused him. He said he wanted to cut off a woman's lips with it.'

'How could you tell he was aroused?'

'He was naked honey.'

'But he never hurt you?'

'No.'

'He laid it on the bed and did the job. I kept staring at it, nervous he'd cut me, but he didn't. Then, as he was leaving I saw a stain on his hand. It looked like dried blood.'

'Did you tell the police?'

'What would they do?'

'And this was ten years ago?'

'Yes. I admire what you do a lot.'

'The police don't.'

'What do they know?

'Is there anything else you can remember?'

'He has a tattoo.'

'Whereabouts?'

'On his chest, it's unusual, never seen one like it, just one word.'

'What word?'

'Lies.'

'Are there any other things he did or said that makes you think he was The Pimp?'

'If there are I can't recall, my memory is cloudy at times.'

'Thank you, you've been extremely helpful.'

Tammy stood up and watched as Joyce got up and stubbed out her cigarette in a glass ashtray.

'I asked him about it once,' Joyce said.

'The tattoo?'

'He said he'd had it done because of something that happened.'

'Something that happened to him?'

'He wouldn't say, but I'm guessing. He said, "Your kind are all liars to the whoring bone," nice use of words he had.'

'Your kind meaning escorts?'

'Meaning women. He said all women were liars and he wanted to take away the thing that let them lie and remain pretty, because without desire they were nothing.'

'He was talking about their mouths.'

'He was. And I hear this killer cuts their lips off.'

'Sometimes the tongues too.'

Joyce came close to her and lowered her voice, as if what she was about to say was too humiliating, even in the privacy of her home.

'He did one thing, once at the end, and I'll never forget it.'

'What did he do?'

'He told me to close my eyes and open my mouth and he'd pay me double. I did, I needed the money, I had a drug problem back then. You have to understand the life I used to lead. I was naked and he touched me, he put the fingers of one hand inside me and with his other hand he slid something across my lips and shut my mouth on it. He squeezed my chin and jaw together and rubbed me below. When he let go of me I spat it out.'

'What did he put in your mouth?'

'A ragged piece of flesh, pink and bruised, I could tell that it had once been part of a woman's mouth.'

'From what we know he's only been killing for two years.'

'Oh, he's been doing it longer.'

'Why do you say that?'

'A man like that, he had to have been killing, I think you've only known about him for two years. He used to tell me I needed a pimp, I never had one you see.'

Joyce showed her to the door. As Tammy opened it Joyce touched her arm with the fondness of an aunt. She looked up at her with wistful, wounded eyes.

'You're a nice looking lady, do you have a boyfriend?'

'Not at the moment.'

'If you ever feel like company.'

'If you think of anything else please call me.'

'I might just do that.'

'What did his voice sound like?'

'Like someone speaking from inside a steel cage. Like ice and frozen metal.'

'That's him all right,' Tammy said.

'He said a whore without a pimp was like a mouth without lips.'

'Where did he used to visit you?'

'I worked in Soho.'

'What time of the day did he used to visit you?'

'Late afternoons mostly, sometimes earlier.'

'I'm trying to figure out if he worked nearby.'

'He might have done, but then he could have seen me on days off, he also said he quit his job, wanted to be his own boss, wanted to be mine, would help me get more customers.'

'You recall what he said in great detail.'

'A man like that, yes, he stains you, being inside me even with what I did, he made me feel filthy, as if I was exposed to some criminal disease that he transmits sexually.'

Tammy looked at Joyce's mouth, at the fullness of her lips and then glanced over her shoulder. There was a line of detergents on the floor in the hallway in a neat row by the skirting board. Joyce kissed her on the cheek and Tammy smelled her perfume rising from her skin, a subtle aroma of morning glory and summer flowers that died on the surfactant odour that overwhelmed the house, as if Joyce had washed away both pleasure and sin to cleanse herself of the past. The maroon lipstick on Joyce's mouth looked darker, as if she had freshly applied another layer, and her lips seemed to be weeping blood as Tammy turned and stepped out into the furnace of heat, glancing back once to see

Joyce watching her, her face harrowed, lost, her eyes broken and locked on the image of an inner violation.

3

People said that Julius Gold shone. With his indigo eyes and his tight, athletic physique he was a guy who looked as though he'd stepped straight from the pages of a fashion magazine. His face was tanned, not too deeply, but an olive colour, and he had a blonde fire about him. Then there was his great dress sense. He liked to wear a mix of tailored clothes and designer gear. He was always classy in an erotic, laid back way, different from the rest. His women sometimes called him Jules, stretching the sound out and thinking of diamonds, and all the expensive things they liked to wear on their skin. Wealthy women loved it when he'd involve their jewellery in their sessions. They loved what he did with his tongue. They called him all sorts of things when he made love to them. They sometimes called him Caesar, for fun.

That evening he was sitting in Attic, the exclusive and glamorous bar set on the 48th floor of Pan Peninsula in Canary Wharf. The London sky was a deep polished blue beyond the shining windows and Julius stared down at the financial district, as lights came on like stars. He liked to frequent Attic because he thought the view of London spread out like a million glistening jewels below was an aphrodisiac to the women who came there. And they came, all the young models and the well adorned wives of the wealthy businessmen away on trips, allowing disinterest to give their wives free reign to roam, they came, all the talent spotting, available, hungry and louche women who wanted a little excitement in their secret lives. For that is where he lived, in secrecy and hidden meetings. Julius was part of the twilit world of erotic assignations.

He was sipping his Chardonnay, rich, full bodied, from Argentina, tasting of apricot, when he spotted her walking in. She was five four and with a great figure, beautiful brown hair, deep brown eyes, and a full mouth. He could see her clearly against the backdrop of the burning sky, fumbling in her handbag.

She didn't see him at first. Karen Sincere was nervous, thinking the bar wasn't her, feeling out of place, thinking her heels were wrong, not a good match for the short black skirt she'd picked out after two glasses of wine. Then she saw Julius sitting at the bar and she changed her mind. She only had that evening, she told herself. Her husband Micky was away and it was the only chance she had to steal a little something back from her poisoned life. Julius was looking at her and she held his gaze and counted two seconds, then looked away, walked over to the side of the bar and ordered a Pinot Grigio, glancing at her reflection in the mirror, liking the blouse now, light blue, showing just enough cleavage, and the hint of the black bra she had on, her favourite La Senza, the one Micky didn't like her to wear.

She watched him in the mirror. He was still looking, checking her out, this young spunk there on the stool, almost within arm's reach. She'd heard about this place. She sipped from her glass, thinking the wine was good. Julius got off his stool, walked over to her and offered her his hand. She stood there looking at it, waiting for him to speak, then she touched his skin.

'I don't suppose you'd join me,' he said.

'Do I know you?'

'Perhaps not. My friend has an appointment and can't make it.'

'Friend?'

'He and I go way back, so I'm not annoyed in the least, especially if my evening turns out the way I hope it will.'

'Oh, and what way is that?'

'Enjoying your company, if you'll be my guest.'

Karen thought it wasn't corny the way he said it, maybe because his voice sounded like treacle and she wanted him already.

'We haven't been introduced.'

'Julius Gold,' he said.

'And what do you do, Julius, apart from pick women up in bars?'

'I'm not a roué, if that's what you think.'

'You're unusual, I'll give you that.'

'May I ask your name?'

'Karen Sincere.'

'And are you sincere?'

'Sometimes, it all depends.'

'On what?'

'The company I'm in.'

She joined him at a table and sat looking out at the view, London below them, all her troubles a million miles away, just her and this handsome man she began to crave as she ate. They had smoked salmon, tiny pieces but so good, sunblushed tomatoes, bar snacks tastefully presented and all with a twist of something in them she hadn't had before at the restaurants Micky took her to while he talked of work. She chewed slowly, listening to Julius, loving his voice more and more over the wine.

'You can see the Gherkin,' he said.

'It looks good from up here, but then I find everything does from a distance.'

'It sounds like you're trying to escape from something.'

'Somebody,' she said.

'Are you married Karen?'

He said it without hesitation and she liked him for that, getting straight to the point, the reason she was there.

'I am,' she said, looking at her ring finger.

She'd taken it off before she left, but now she didn't need to lie, she could be honest with this guy, and as she thought that, she knew what was going to happen that night, knew it all the way to the iron bed posts she wrapped her hands around as he entered her on silk sheets.

They left beneath a clear sky that spoke of summer, only of summer and heat, and he drove her to his flat in Kew in a convertible Audi that was whiter than snow and left several cars standing at the bright red lights. She liked his place, modern, clean, tastefully designed, a few abstracts hanging on the pastel coloured walls, artists whose names she didn't know.

She wanted him to touch her, standing there with a glass of Pinot Noir. She wanted to experience him before the night died and she returned home to Micky and his lies. And he did, gently, his hand on her arm, his amazing eyes on hers as she began to get more aroused than she'd ever known.

Then he pressed his lips to hers and she wrapped her slender arms around his neck. They went into the bedroom where he unwrapped her like a prize, slowly exploring her body in the erotic night. She felt feverish, high on him, and young again. And as he touched her Karen thought 34 wasn't too old. She looked great and she knew it, especially when she got away from Micky. Yes she looked good, she thought, glancing at her tits as he removed her bra. No sag, no work, none needed. She kept in shape, worked out, now he was taking off her G-string, sliding it down her legs slowly.

He did it all to her, this man straight from her fantasies. It was as if he knew what she craved and he gave it to her. His body was even better than she'd imagined at the bar when she tried to picture him without his clothes. He was muscled but not overly so, she always hated that body builder look.

The way he touched her was an instant turn on. And she laid back on the bed and had it all that stolen night.

She forgot about Micky as he made love to her. But afterwards she began to feel afraid, for this one night stand troubled her deeply, because she wanted more of him.

4

Tammy Wayne was sitting in her white terry cotton bathrobe at her house in Fulham, drinking a cup of coffee, a deep Italian roast, when she heard the letterbox rattle. She went out into the hall. There was no mail, and she opened the door, glanced at the deserted street and stared down at the box that sat on the mat. She took it inside and laid it on the kitchen table. The box looked like any small parcel, typed address, standard cardboard. Hand delivered. She removed the sellotape that held it together, opened it, and pulled out the tissue paper. Then she ran to the bathroom where she knelt on the cold tiles and retched into the toilet.

She stood and dabbed at her face with a wet flannel wondering how he knew her address. She'd been so careful. Then she composed herself, went back into the kitchen and looked at it. She should have known he'd send it. The Pimp never threatened anything he didn't carry through.

She wanted to cry, she wanted to shoot him, she wanted to stay calm, but all she really wanted was her sister back. It had been two years and he must have kept them on ice. She thought of what he'd said about frozen skin on the phone. And she realised that the rape and mutilation of her sister would be re-enacted on her again and again.

Because the man who'd delivered the box to her doorstep wasn't content with murder, he wanted it to live on in the hearts and minds of the relatives, he wanted to sear it into your consciousness with acid until he inhabited you like a savage wraith. To The Pimp all women were whores, and brutality was a professional necessity. And what he'd given Tammy was a lust to kill him. For she hungered for it so breathlessly at times it was as if hatred and arousal had become fused in her body.

There on her kitchen table at the bottom of the box were Holly's lips. He'd left the diamond stud piercing in it, the one Tammy had bought her for her last Christmas when she looked so beautiful and fragile. Tammy had known she was working as a stripper and kept her concern about her lifestyle to herself. She had a beautiful mouth. As Tammy gazed at it she saw something jutting through the surface of the upper lip. She bent and peered at it. It was green and spiked. It took everything she had to lift Holly's mouth up with the end of a Bic biro. Then she saw it, The Pimp's piece of humour. He'd pierced her lips with a holly leaf.

Tammy jumped as her mobile phone rang on the table. She picked it up and glanced at caller ID. Private number. She hesitated, then answered.

'Tammy Wayne.'

'I bet you just want to kiss it don't you?' The Pimp said.

She'd expected the call, but not here at home on her mobile. He was gathering more information on her than she thought possible.

'You can't disturb me that easily,' Tammy said.

'You think I want to disturb you?'

'These little games are going to come to an end.'

'I sent you her mouth because I want you to have a good picture of her saying it.'

'Saying what?'

There was a pause, then she heard Holly's desperate, pleading voice.

'Please don't do this, I'm pregnant, you're killing two people. What have I done to you, if you want money my sister's got money.'

The recording ended there. Tammy felt as though he was turning a rusted corkscrew round and round inside her heart.

'You see it was never about money,' The Pimp said. 'You didn't know she was pregnant did you?'

'When I catch up with you you're going to regret this.'

'I've evidently upset you, you're such a fragile little thing underneath all that butch machismo you like to sport. I took that recording shortly before I slit her lips from her face, the cheap little whore, I bet you're a cheap whore in bed too, I might just check you out before I do you.'

'I bet a man like you can't get a woman. You need to use prostitutes don't you?'

'Have you been talking to that aging slut Joyce? Her mouth was only ever fit for one thing.'

This threw Tammy, his knowing she'd gone to speak to Joyce.

'Your bombs didn't work.'

'I don't use bombs as you know.'

'The two at my office, I was out at the time.'

'Talking to a fellow hooker. Did you swap cock stories?'

'I'm going to find you.'

'Well then you'll lose your mouth.'

'What is it with you and mouths?'

'I like collecting lips.'

'Who else would want to blow me up?'

'You must have enemies. You track killers, there are a lot of them about.'

'You're the only person I can think of who would do that.'

'But I didn't and you know it.'

She didn't want to believe him, but she did. He would have been outside watching the building if he'd planted the explosives, and he wouldn't have detonated them if he knew she'd gone out, so it was someone else. Tammy's brain raced for an explanation, an idea of who might have done it, and she felt as though she'd stepped over a coastal shelf into a predatory world with no limits.

'She stripped for me, put on a show, jiggled those tits of hers, not bad for a slut. She had a diamond in her navel, I carved a scar into her eyes with it.'

'You make tools don't you?'

'You've just lost Joyce her lips. Tammy, you need to brag, you probably like it on top, but you'll never get on top of a man like me.'

'Right now the police are watching her house, waiting for you to show.'

'Do you know what she said, that sister of yours?'

'Are you afraid of what women say about you, did someone put you down, is that why you have this thing for mouths?'

'She said she'd do anything sexually if I let her go.'

'Why do you call yourself The Pimp?'

'Because I get the women for him.'

'Who?'

'He's at my house, he's waiting for you, Tammy. He will eat your flesh, you will fuck him before you die just like Holly did, she took him right inside her.'

'Who is this, your accomplice?'

'I'm performing a service you see, I get him his whores then I take their lips away.'

'Every sick serial killer like you has to dress his perversions up.'

'I have to take their lips away because they can't speak about him.'

'Who?'

'You know, Tammy, you know deep down who he is, and you want him, you want to feel him inside you.'

'No, it's you and your sickness.'

'I like your bathrobe, it matches the pallor of your expression this fine summer morning, feeling a little bilious are you?'

She spun round and looked out of the window at the front garden. The road outside was empty apart from her Mercedes.

'Looking for me Tammy? Come and get me, but you better be prepared, take that gun with you, hold it like a cock.'

'Oh I'm coming for you and when I catch you I'm going to empty the magazine into your head.'

She picked her Glock up from her holster that was hanging from the back of a chair and raced out onto the front path. She had bare feet and stepped onto broken glass, gashing her soles as she scanned the street. But there was nobody there, only the paper boy who paused and stared at her as he handed her the local paper with a look of embarrassment.

Tammy took it and went inside, leaving bloody foot prints on her tiles. She picked her mobile phone up from the table.

'If you've got a camera rigged up outside I'll find it,' she said.

'I'd see a doctor if I were you, I contaminated that glass.'

'You keep playing your sick little games.'

'I did it while you were in the bath,' The Pimp said.

'You might be watching me but you don't know half as much as you pretend to.'

'You used a Remington trimmer on the blonde hair on your pudenda, then you masturbated after you lathered yourself up, I bet you thought of me.'

'You know I'm going to get you.'

'Turn to the centre fold, and pull your robe together, you're giving me a nipple shot.'

The line went dead and Tammy glanced down to see how far her robe had parted. She pulled it to and opened the Fulham Gazette.

Inserted next to an article about surveillance was a naked picture of Holly. She had her arms tethered to two steel chains and a knife was poised against her mouth.

Across her breasts The Pimp had scrawled the words, 'She thought I was after her pussy but I just wanted her lips.' Tammy put on some socks and went out into the street to find the paper boy, to ask him who had tampered with her paper. But he was gone, and the street was empty. Then she went into the bathroom to tend to her bleeding feet.

5

Karen stayed for breakfast, knowing Micky wouldn't be back until the afternoon. She watched her lover make it as she pushed her life away. Julius gave her fresh coffee, standing in the kitchen in his jockeys, Karen loving the way he moved, so natural, as she thought about the night. He made bacon sandwiches, it was what she wanted, rare for her to have something so filling first thing. But she was hungry.

'I want to see you again,' she said.

'If your husband allows you out of the house.'

'How can you tell? You discern so much about me.'

'I know the look.'

'He controls me and he watches me.'

'You sound afraid of him.'

'I am.'

'Is he violent to you?'

'Sometimes,' she hesitated then, wanting to make the admission she'd kept to herself, feeling now here she could say it. 'I think he's leading a double life.'

'As what?'

'A killer.'

Julius turned those mesmerising eyes on her. She drifted a while from the thought of it, her fears about Micky, his latent darkness, she wanted Julius to take her through to the bedroom and take it all away again. Instead they talked, and she told him some of the things she'd been so afraid of for months at the big gated house in Sheen with the dogs and the pain.

'What makes you think that?' Julius said.

'It's really odd, I never thought I'd be sitting here telling you or anyone about it.'

'It sounds to me as though you need to talk. Does he go away a lot?'

'Yes, and he always returns different. Micky builds up this tension inside him, he works long hours, and in bed, he's, well, almost violent with me. Sometimes I think he hates me, then he takes one of his trips, they're never long, he's on one now, and he returns calmer. I did think he was seeing another woman but that's not it.'

'That would be the logical explanation.'

'But it's not, I checked his clothes and found something.'

'What?'

'Blood on his shirt. And a weapon, a long handled boning knife covered in blood.'

6

Tammy went to her doctor in a mini cab, her feet hurting her too much to drive. She had a private doctor, a woman called Marjorie Tram, she'd been seeing her for years. When Tammy called, her receptionist said she'd had a cancellation and she gave Tammy the slot. Dr Tram listened to Tammy's account of how she'd received the injuries. She was a good-looking woman, blonde, natural look, cute beneath her half-moon glasses, and Tammy felt a little flutter pass through her as she bent and looked over the rims at her and touched her feet, inspecting the wounds. Tammy had always felt an attraction to her that she'd pushed away, another woman was not her style, but that morning as sunlight blasted through the windows into the office she succumbed, just a little, to the pleasure of her touch as she listened to her calming voice.

'The cuts aren't deep. I'll take a blood test to be sure, I can rush it through to the lab,' Dr Tram said. 'I'll give you a tetanus shot. You're lucky I had a late cancellation.'

Tammy rolled up the sleeve of her blouse and as the needle entered her skin she thought of Holly and the sharp pointed leaf that pierced her dead mouth.

Tammy was drifting, thinking of Holly, of how much she loved her sister, how beautiful she was, better than all the boyfriends she had and who never valued her.

'If the glass was contaminated what could he have used?' Tammy said.

'Any number of things.'

'How lethal could they be?'

'It's hard to get hold of the really lethal toxins, and handling them is extremely dangerous so we can eliminate quite a lot of them.'

Tammy stood up, feeling lightheaded.

'You'll call me when the result comes through?'

'Later today. I know what you went through with your sister, but don't you think it's best leaving it to the police?'

'They're not going to catch him.'

'How can you be so sure?'

'They closed the case. They said it was the work of a man called Gerald Yard, who was shot in a police stake out. He had two freezers full of female body parts at his house. He told the police he admired The Pimp, but he had a psychiatric record of a split personality and a number of assumed identities. They believe he was The Pimp.'

'And you don't, Tammy?'

'I'm getting calls from him, he sent me my sister's lips in the post.'

Dr Tram took a deep breath.

'Report it to the police.'

'When the calls started I did. They're didn't take me seriously, they treated me like some obsessed relative wasting their time. I'm the only person who's going to catch him.'

'And what if he catches you?'

'I served in the Royal Artillery, I'm good at finding people.'

'Go home and rest, I'll call later with the test result.'

Tammy did, she lay on the sofa and thought about that morning's events and how much The Pimp knew. She went over what Joyce had told her. She knew that the fact he visited her in Soho was not a lead. It was too long ago, and he may have lied about his life. And as he watched every movement of hers, he evaded all her attempts to locate him. She went into the bathroom and hunted for the camera. She spent two hours checking the walls for holes, signs of recent drilling and fresh paint, the window frame, the air vent, the plugs. She knew all the tricks, all the gadgets used in surveillance.

She got tired, went and made a coffee and a cheese sandwich, then went back in. The Pimp had watched her take a bath, there had to be a camera. His account of her morning was too accurate and she needed to regain her privacy to operate. As she stood there she saw it. So clever. She always kept a tissue box in a container next to the sink. The one she bought was violet, this was darker, not much, but she was convinced it was a replacement.

Tammy put on some latex gloves and took it apart. Within minutes she found the camera and transmitter inside. She'd dust the box for prints, knowing The Pimp was too smart to leave any, but army training kicked in and she was looking for that mistake from him. She tried to figure out when he'd put it there, knowing these devices used batteries that didn't last more than ten hours, and she recalled the late trip the night before to the supermarket and thinking the air in the bathroom felt cold when she returned.

He must have broken in while she was shopping, but he must have been in her house before then, and found out she kept a tissue box in a container by the sink. He was studying her, collecting pieces of her lifestyle. Tammy took the camera out to the kitchen and placed it in a cardboard box. Then she went back into the bathroom to get rid of the tissues she'd removed. As she picked them up she saw a mark, a dark colour beneath the tissue at the top. She lifted it up and stared at a piece of blood stained white cotton. Then her mobile phone rang. She knew who it was before she got to the kitchen and answered it.

'She was wearing white panties, how virginal,' The Pimp said.

'I found the camera.'

'As I knew you would. That's a piece of Holly's panties, they were soiled, I have her bra too and her cheap tights, I have a lot of Holly I'm going to send to you express delivery.'

'You won't be watching me any more.'

'I'll send you something nice, something straight from your fantasies.'

'I know the transmission range of these things, you've got be nearby.'

'You know a few tricks like your sister, but there's a lot you don't know.'

'I know I'm going to catch you.'

'Did you know I kept her blood?'

'That could be anyone's.'

'Test it, I know you will. How are your feet?'

'The camera will have its own internal IP, I'll track you from it.'

'Do you really think I'm that dumb?'

'I think you're worried.'

'Worried about what Tammy?'

'That I'm going to catch you.'

'I know what you felt for her, I don't think it worked both ways.'

'I know what I'm going to do to you when I find you.'

'Shoot me with your Glock?'

'I'll use hollow points.'

'I bet you wished you'd fucked her while she was alive.'

The line went dead. Tammy did call the police, told them that she'd seen a man in her street checking out houses. She said he was about six foot but didn't get a good look at him. She didn't mention her sister, maybe they'd catch him as he staked her out. As she hung up her phone went again. She was relieved to see it was Marjorie Tram on the caller display.

'Good news,' she said, 'there's no contamination, he's playing games with you.'

'Thanks for letting me know.'

She hung up and thought about it. The Pimp could easily have infected the glass, so why didn't he? Because he wanted her out of the house so he could break in. She spent the afternoon looking for more cameras. She didn't find any. She did find that her Glock was missing from the holster on the back of the kitchen chair. Her heart began to hammer in her chest. Tammy had made a decision to break the law when she'd bought it from an army colleague. She wasn't legally allowed to own a handgun, but she needed to be armed. Her belief that The Pimp was going to kill her was something she carried about like a bruise. And she was angry with the police, they'd made her feel neurotic and irrelevant. There were nights when she sat in her bedroom and wondered if she was going insane in her hunt for the man who did those things to Holly. The pain would wake her, the anguish of loss tugging her from feverish dreams, her T-shirt soaked in sweat. She'd rise and pace her house like a troubled guest, feeling distant from her own life, and ask herself what she was doing with a gun. Then she would hear his voice and feel the handle of her Glock in her hand and she could breathe more easily.

She was still looking for it when he called again.

'Your gun's on Joyce's sofa, next to her brains,' he said.

7

Joyce Farmer's cleaner found her body that afternoon. The Pimp had stripped Joyce and blown her head away with Tammy's Glock, but it wasn't at the scene of the crime. Her lips were intact, The Pimp had not used his signature on the woman who'd opened her mouth about him. What he had left was Tammy's business card, perched between Joyce's lips like a bank note jutting out of a vending machine. He'd also left two photographs of Tammy leaving Joyce's house, which he'd pinned to Joyce's breasts. And he'd soaked her in detergents, covering her skin with bleach. The cleaner called the police, who sealed off the living room. They would later find out from their pathology department that Joyce had been raped with a pistol. The Pimp had used Tammy's Glock to violate her before whipping her face with the butt. He'd inserted the muzzle in her mouth and broken two teeth as he did so. He positioned her with her legs apart. Then he smeared soil from her garden across her naked skin. He got her lipstick out of her handback and coated her lips with it.

Tammy wrestled with the idea of calling the police, but she believed it was a trap. She drove round to the address, her feet hurting on the pedals.

She parked at the end of the road as two police officers got out of their car and went inside. She sat there shaking. The gun was unregistered, but if her prints were on it and The Pimp directed the police her way, what then? She drove home and called a debugging company to come and sweep her house.

Two officers visited her at home that evening, Inspector Norman Hunt and Constable Harry Bright. She let them in, offered them coffee, but they declined. She sat on her sofa as they each took a chair opposite and questioned her about the fact that her business card had been found at the murder scene, not mentioning the gun.

'I visited her yesterday,' Tammy said.

'In connection with what?' Hunt said.

She paused and took him in, wondering what she didn't know, whether he was holding back the question about her gun. Hunt was a tall, middle-aged man with small angry eyes, and the flush on his cheek made Tammy wonder if he was a drinker. She sensed the antagonism from the moment he'd walked through the door, guessing he knew about her involvement with the investigation into the murder of her sister. The word the last officer she spoke to used was 'interference,' and she guessed that was how Hunt saw her.

'She'd called me with information about the killer known as The Pimp.'

'I noticed there are some notes about your involvement with this case.'

'Joyce said she knew him. He was a client of hers.'

'A client?'

'She used to be a prostitute.'

'Why do you think your card was inserted in her mouth?'

'He has a thing about lips.'

'This man called The Pimp?'

'Yes, I think he's trying to set me up.'

He looked at his colleague. Harry Bright was in his twenties, Tammy estimated, not bad looking but his face was filled with disdain. And the way he looked at her was making Tammy angry. He'd glanced at her boobs as his senior officer questioned her and smiled to himself.

'Why would he be trying to set you up?' Bright said.

'Because I'm onto him.'

'This theory of yours that he killed your sister.'

'It's not a theory.'

'So you're saying The Pimp killed Joyce Farmer and tried to make it look as though you're implicated,' Hunt said.

'Yes, that's what I'm saying.'

'Sounds a little paranoid to me.'

'If you'd been through what I have, ah, what's the point,' Tammy said standing up.

'And what have you been through?'

'He's been threatening me for months.'

'You haven't reported it.'

'And why do you think that is?'

'You don't have a lot of respect for the police do you Mrs Wayne?' Hunt said.

'Are you going to arrest me?'

'No.'

'Then I have nothing further to say.'

They stood up and Bright glanced at her legs.

'There were two photographs of you outside Joyce Farmer's house, pinned to her breasts,' Bright said.

'He must have taken them, he's got me under surveillance.'

'He's covered her with soil. He'd written something on the back of your card in bright blue felt tip, "you can't get a soiled whore clean, but you can cover their lies with lipstick."'

'When are you going to start taking me seriously?'

'We're taking this murder extremely seriously, Ms Wayne.'

'Are you going to try to find The Pimp?'

'Do you know why we're not going to arrest you?' Hunt said.

'Because you know I didn't kill her.'

'A neighbour saw the killer enter the building.'

'Who did the neighbour see?'

'We can't discuss that.'

'The Pimp killed Joyce.'

'The case you're talking about is closed, the killer is in prison.'

'It's not Gerald Yard.'

'We'll be in touch if we have more questions.'

They left and she watched them walk down her path and get into their car. They hadn't mentioned her gun, and Tammy felt relief wash across her body. It didn't last for long as she immediately began to wonder what The Pimp's latest game was. She could almost feel his breath on her neck as she tried to analyse his motives. Tammy was sure he'd used her Glock. He used something of hers to kill a woman, but it wasn't her the police were looking for. He was giving her a warning: don't try to find me or you will get women killed. But also he was showing her how easily he could move in and out of her life, taunting her.

The man Joyce Farmer's neighbour saw leaving was tall and lean and wore a long coat. He was an ex-client of hers named Herbert Reed. He'd become obsessed by Joyce and found out her address and had been turning up demanding sex. The neighbour, an elderly women called Dora Fiddle, who sat by her curtains all day watching the street, had seen him twice. On this occasion Dora saw him standing in the street yelling up at Joyce's window. Joyce let him in, concerned what he would say in the street which might be overheard by her neighbour. Reed didn't shut the door as he walked in. Joyce took him into her living room and tried explaining she was retired. Reed became aggressive and grabbed her shoulder. Then Joyce saw another man enter her living room. He slammed a piece of lead pipe down on Herbert Reed's head then silenced her by covering her mouth with his leather gloved hand. She knew him, she'd known him years ago, this tool maker come to show her not to open her mouth. He gagged her with duct tape before he raped her with Tammy's gun. He used a silencer to shoot her before he left with Reed.

Dora hadn't seen him come or go because she'd taken a call. The Pimp saw her walk away from the window before he went in. He knew the layout of her house, he'd disengaged the phone in the room that looked out onto the street, and he knew that Dora would have to go to a back room on the first floor to take the call. He knew Dora was trying to get compensation from the Inland Revenue, who she claimed had overcharged her. The caller kept her on the phone while The Pimp killed Joyce and left, asking Dora the relevant questions and then ending the call by saying she would be getting a cheque in the post when he received a text message from The Pimp. The caller had a raspy voice. When he hung up, The Pimp was a mile away, with Reed's body in the back of his van. He'd backed it onto Joyce Farmer's drive and bundled Reed into the back.

The Pimp knew he wasn't being watched, he knew Dora was taking the call, he knew the neighbours on the other side of Joyce's house were at work, as were those opposite. No one could see the back of his van. Besides, he wore shades and a hat when he went into Joyce's house and when he came out of it. The Pimp knew all about the road Joyce lived in. It had been fun killing her, he wanted to take her lips with him so badly, but he needed to be careful. He thought about Tammy, picturing her mouth as he drove Reed to the countryside, taking in the green fields outside his window.

As he parked, Hunt was ringing Reed's doorbell. They knew about his assaults on prostitutes. This would be easy. They'd interviewed him before, and knew it was only a matter of time before he killed someone. Hunt took a step back and glanced up at his windows, turning to Bright, who stood on the pavement.

'Looks like he's not in,' Hunt said.

'They never are when you need them to be.'

As Hunt and Bright walked away Reed was sitting in a chair in a bare windowless room. He was naked and bound with leathers straps. He glanced to his right as a steel door opened and tall man wearing a leather apron and fisherman's boots walked in. At first he thought his abductor's face was deformed, he seemed to have a purple patch the colour of a plum running across his skin. Then he saw that he was wearing a mask of a huge pair of lips. The man in the mask lifted a two foot piece of steel girder from a work bench. The ends were as sharp as a butcher's knife. He swung it back, then he rammed the sharpened ends into Reed's chest.

8

The house in Sheen stood behind security gates fronted by a long gravel drive. It held seven bedrooms, four bathrooms, two living rooms, an office, a pool room, a swimming pool and a sound proofed building at the back of the garden where Micky shot guns. His lifestyle existed like a wound in the road of bankers and well to do middle class families. He invited businessmen of a dubious background round to dinner parties from which he excluded his neighbours.

That evening Micky was late. Karen had been thinking she could have stayed longer with Julius if she'd known, in fact she'd done little else than think about Julius. The dogs Micky kept, Dobermans and Rottweilers, two of each, were chained to an iron fence at the back of the house. Karen didn't like feeding them, she didn't like their teeth. They responded to Micky and only Micky. He used them at times. She'd seen him set them on a business colleague one summer night. She never forget the marks they left in his legs or the mirth in Micky's eyes as he pulled them off him. No one ripped her husband off, especially her. They existed in a canine word that promised retribution to her if she strayed, and Karen felt they were watching her, studying her movements for abnormalities. When Micky was at home he would take them for long walks in Richmond Park, alone always alone. Karen often wondered if they would protect her if an intruder broke in. She felt they were there to create an air of constant menace, to uphold the threat that Micky exerted. She was enjoying a glass of Pinot Grigio looking at the rain fall outside the window when she heard Micky come in.

'Have you been behaving yourself?' he said, striding into the living room.

He brought with him the smell of ozone and aftershave, and Karen wondered if it was the summer sky that had soaked his clothes, or whether it was something else, something he had done that she was smelling on the black sports jacket he took off and placed on the chair next to her, standing over her, waiting for her greeting.

'What's that supposed to mean?' she said.

Micky adjusted his belt, gripping the worn leather with his fists and running his fingertips across the chrome buckle that was shaped like a letter 'M' as Karen looked at him. He was a good-looking man, with a clean complexion and even features, but the scar that ran down one side of his face undermined his appeal. It rose from the surface of his skin like a red welt, and gave the appearance that his face was starting to split, as if it echoed the inner dislocation of his character, one prone to savagery and sexual corruption, as Karen knew all too well. Mick told her held got it in a knife fight in a pub when they first met. He added that he did more than scar the other fellow.

The reality of Julius and his touch began to fade as Micky stood there, bringing with him all his rage. It existed in his gestures and his facial expression like a stain on the physical made by his sexual thoughts. His eyes burned with anger. And Karen dreaded what he would ask from her, knowing now that she had found a lover Micky's erotic demands would be more painful than before, when she had known no contrast or relief. He walked over to her and reached for the bottle of wine that sat on a table next to the chair she was sitting on. Then he got a glass from the bar and poured himself one.

'What it means is what have you been up to? Have you done anything I should know about?' he said.

'Only shopping.'

'Only shopping,' Micky said, nodding and knocking back the wine.

He wiped his mouth with the back of his hand, and filled her glass. He watched her drink it, saying nothing, then he reached down and grabbed her arm.

'Ow, that hurts Micky, let go.'

'You know the procedure.'

'What, now?'

'Now.'

'You normally return in a good mood from your trips.'

'I am in a good mood. Stand beneath the light.'

'You know you've got nothing to worry about.'

'Then neither have you.'

Micky folded his arms as Karen began to undress. She expected this, he did it on occasions. She'd showered when she got home and put the clothes she wore the night before in the wash. Julius hadn't left a mark on her, Micky wouldn't find what he was looking for. She undid her blouse, unzipped her skirt, then slipped out of her heels, unhooking her bra and sliding down her G-string. Micky ran his hands across her skin. He stared at every inch of her. Then he stood back.

'Can I get dressed now?' Karen said.

'After we've gone upstairs.'

Karen complied, wearily climbing the large staircase to the bedroom.

It was brief and perfunctory. Micky undid his belt and entered her without ceremony on the bed, spent himself inside her, then stood and zipped up his fly. He hadn't bothered to undress. But as Karen lay beneath him, locked in her despair at the proximity of his body to hers she kept smelling his aftershave, wondering if she was using the olfactory sensation to distract her from the torment she felt. After he left the room and wandered into the hallway, she thought it was more than that, as if the smell contained another odour, more than testosterone and hate, less than oil and alcohol, the perfume of the dangerous man, his thoughts leaking through his skin and collecting in his pores like blood seeping from a ruptured vein.

She rose and looked at him beneath the light in the hall, and Micky turned, his green eyes as hard as emeralds in his face. Karen felt exposed and she drew her arms across her body and realised she was shaking. It was as if the night with Julius had peeled a layer of skin away and now she lived with the raw bruise of her marriage. And as she returned his invasive gaze she asked herself who was it she had married all those years ago when she was young and Micky was charming and kind. She felt robbed and her heart ached for the past when she felt like a wife not the occasional object of a brutality whose source she could not define. She began to dress hurriedly, like a teenager caught in the act by a stern father, her skin cold to the touch, her palms clammy. And Micky watched her with a tiny smile on his face, nodding, as if she was making a statement with which he agreed.

Then he came into the room. Karen was trying to button her blouse but her fingers were shaking.

'Don't tell me you didn't like it,' he said.

'I wouldn't lie to you Micky.'

'You need to see a doctor.'

'Stop playing games with me.'

He took her right hand and lowered it to her thigh. She was standing in her blouse, the buttons done up hallway, her skirt in her left hand. Below her black G-string was a dark patch and Micky rubbed her palm across it. Karen looked down and failed to comprehend what it was until he told her, as if she was a child who needed everything explained to her.

'You're bleeding.'

'It's not my time.'

'It's a nasty gash, you're a brave girl.'

'Did you do that to me?'

Karen reached for his belt and began to undo it, then she felt the prong slash her fingers. It was as sharp as a razor, filed to a point like a needle.

9

The debugging company arrived nice and early. They swept Tammy's house and found only one camera in the kitchen, hidden in the handle of a cupboard. The Pimp had watched Tammy with it as she took his call with her bathrobe open. He saw her Glock hanging in her holster from the back of the chair. As she looked at the tiny camera she thought of all the times she'd wandered into the kitchen naked and of The Pimp's description of her in the bath. Tammy felt violated, as if a faceless stranger had raped her in her sleep. She was enclosed in a world of surveillance, chasing a man with no identity apart from the one shaped from the deeds he horrified her with. Being watched, and to be unable to see who was watching her, was beginning to make her feel part of an act of pornography.

After the company left, she went and bought a replacement Glock from her army colleague, another 21. She liked the gun, liked its weight in her palm and the action as it fired and she longed to empty its magazine into The Pimp's head. As she drove home, dodging the traffic, cutting through lights that were turning red, she smelled cordite rising from the barrel and felt aroused as she determined she would find him and end him.

That afternoon she looked for another office in Fulham. She found one that was a few blocks away from her old office. It was smaller, but had good CCTV footage of the outside of the building as well as the hallways, and she could move in immediately. Tammy decided she was not going to advertise the address.

The office consisted of two rooms, one with a desk and chair. She ordered some extra furniture and then set about dealing with the latest emails from clients. Tammy specialised in tracking down killers, usually men who had kidnapped people for ransom. This was easy work to her, easy compared to trying to catch The Pimp, whose elusiveness and expertise at surveillance left her with a begrudging admiration. She'd often thought he was ex-military to be so good, but there was no information about who he was.

Tammy left the army when Holly was killed. She'd set up her company, Tracking Homicide, to finance her hunt for The Pimp. And she was good at it. Time and again she came across men and women who'd been let down by the police and came to her. And she enjoyed the work, delivering justice in a world where there was little to be found. But it was a substitute for what she really wanted, the end of the man who had tortured and killed Holly.

She'd spent hours analysing The Pimp. And the only information she had was what Joyce had given her. She was looking for a man who made tools. As Tammy sat in her new office, a black Ford lingered on the opposite side of the street. It had been following her all day, and finally when she went home it stopped at the end of her road. The driver watched as she paused at her front door and picked up a parcel. He could see her as she entered the hallway and went into the kitchen.

Tammy put the package down on the table and opened it. Inside, lying on snow white tissue paper were a pair of earrings skewered through two severed earlobes.

10

7:00 PM.

Karen was standing under a bus shelter in the rain when she called Julius.

'I want to see you again, but I have to wait until he goes away,' she said.

'How have you been?'

'I loathe him, Julius. I hate it when he touches me.'

'Leave him.'

'He'd never let me get away. I need to see you, I need to sleep with you.'

'When is he going on another trip?'

'I don't know, he announces it at the last minute.'

'Call me when he does.'

She almost asked him if there were other women, but she felt foolish and didn't want to know.

'He normally goes away twice a month.'

'Then he's due for one,' Julius said.

She said goodbye and drove home. She craved him more and more and her loathing for her husband was growing inside her like an unremitting ache. She'd tried to understand why she hadn't felt the prong of his belt cut her thigh that night. She'd asked herself had he spiked her drink. But Micky offered no explanation, nor did her attempts to go over what had happened. The gash on her leg and the cuts on her fingers were healing. But the memory of him on top of her brought with it a feeling of degradation that was as familiar as her own rapid heartbeat whenever he approached her for sex. She remembered how her heart fluttered when Julius first touched her. It was strange, Micky made her heart race in fear and Julius in pleasure. As the gates to her home closed upon her, the sound of the gravel hitting the sides of her Mercedes sounded like tacks being hammered into a metal sheet.

That night Micky watched from the bedroom as she stepped out of the shower. Karen could see him standing by the lamp in a pair of crisply pressed deep blue trousers and a thin white shirt, his sleeves rolled up as if he was about to engage in a fist fight. She wrapped a towel around her body, seeing his eyes on her, deprecating, flickering with the latent cruelty of his mind. Karen walked into the bedroom and began picking clothes out of a drawer as Micky came up behind her and put his hand on her shoulder. She dreaded the request, the demand for sex, and she feared what he would do if she declined. But Micky didn't ask her to lie down, he removed a panatela from his shirt pocket, and pulled a box of Swan Vesta matches from his trousers. He struck a match and as he raised it to the end of the cigar, the flash of orange reflected in his eyes and Karen thought of melting glass. His nipples were outlined against his shirt. Micky raised the cigar and held it close to her cheek.

'I'm taking a trip tomorrow,' he said.
'How long?'

But he didn't answer her. He put his face close to hers, and she thought he was going to kiss her cheek. But he put his tongue inside her ear then stood back and licked his lips. Then he began to undo his belt, wrapping it around his clenched fist as he took a deep drag on the cigar.

'I suppose you think I'm going to hit you with this,' he said.

'You sharpened it deliberately.'

'Everything's a weapon Karen.'

'No it's not, Micky. You turned that prong into a spike and pressed it into my thigh.'

'Do you think you don't use sex as a weapon?'

'I don't want it much of the time.'

'And why is that?'

'Because you hurt me.'

'Or is it because of something else?'

'Do you think I like being cut?'

'Maybe you're seeing someone.'

'I'm not.'

'So you say but you still don't like feeding the dogs.'

'They're savage.'

'You think I'm savage.'

'That buckle didn't come like that.'

'How do you know?'

'You showed it to me.'

'Did I?'

'Yes, and you made the prong as sharp as a razor so it could cut me.'

'Why do you think I had it made?'

'Because it's the first letter of your name.'

'It doesn't stand for Micky.'

'What does it stand for?'

'Midnight, Karen.'

He turned the light off and left her standing there in the darkness, watching his retreating back in the halo of light shed from the hall.

That night as Micky slept, she called Julius, downstairs in the pool room. But she got his voicemail and hung up.

Julius was chatting to a 28 year old model called Kitten Rogers, her professional name, in another bar in another part of town. She was telling him about her modelling career and Julius was playing it just the way she wanted, giving her all the attention. Later she took him to her flat in Shepherd's Bush, telling him she liked living there, a central and happening place with not too many old people.

Kitten looked stunning, hazel eyes, long lashes, big boobs, natural, she didn't need the work, and long legs she used to tell guys reached all the way to eternity. Julius watched as she bent and did a few lines of coke on a mirror that sat on a glass table surrounded by magazines showing the polished faces of the beautiful crowd she hung with, this young thing showing him enough thigh to get him excited, so she thought. But she knew there was something different here in this man she'd pulled, or had he pulled her, she wondered briefly before the coke burnt its path through her system and took away her doubts, the few she had, and which she tucked under her pillow on the rare occasion she felt them. Ashley lived in a world of sexual certainty. This night would go the way they all did, with her harnessing the male body to her beauty. She thought of what she would do in bed. She looked for desire in his eyes, that tacit signal she could take charge. Then he touched her, in the gentle twilight of her living room, making her shiver as he did. She liked to steer her men, she liked to be boss, but now she wasn't sure of where this was going. This guy was too sure of himself, maybe he wasn't in bed, she'd find out soon enough, she knew that look, she knew where it was heading.

Julius took her upstairs and undressed her, and she felt her control sliding away on the coke and the erotic sensations his hands were inducing in her skin, alive, wanting more than she'd ever known. It was like some sexual ad she was in now, her and this stud about to do it. He looked so good, so assured, it gave her a thrill.

'What's your real name?' he said.

'Pussy.'

'OK Kitten. Or shall I call you Miss Rogers?'

'It's Ashley Greene, but you can call me what you want Julius, are you well hung?'

He touched her in ways she'd never known except in her fantasies, that private world she escaped to after long shoots or sex sessions that left her feeling empty and alone. He peeled her clothes away and kissed her mouth, taking his time, and she found out the answer to her question when she reached into his trousers and gasped with pleasure and a delight that made her feel light headed and breathless. She lay down and he used his tongue and fingers as she arched her back on the bed and wrapped her slender fingers around the bed posts, wanting him to dominate her and wondering why, she never usually did.

Julius kissed her and she pressed her body to his, feeling his skin against hers, his hardness against her thigh. Then he entered her as she wrapped her lean legs around his waist and he was deep inside her and she was tasting the night and all its erotic unshackling. She came twice, then she got on top of him and let her blonde hair cascade across his face like a curtain as she rode him, bending down and putting her tongue in his mouth, moving slowly at first, teasing him, then moving faster, waiting for it. But Julius held out, he held out for hours. And this living fantasy fetched from a bar began to make her feel afraid. She needed to extract his pleasure from him. And as she wrestled for it on the tangled sheets she briefly felt her feminine self-assurance fade like ink in water. She was bent right over him, her nipples brushing his mouth, when he let it go inside her and she took it all, all the way to her need for the kind of attention this man gave, and how, making her feel she was the only one, and that her appeal was endless.

'Are you going to stay the night or am I going to have to cuff you to the bed so you're there in the morning?' she said.

'A woman like you doesn't need to use force for her pleasures, even her secret ones.'

'And what do you know about women like me?'

'I think my hands told you that just now.'

'And what are my secret pleasures?'

'All the things you hide between Kitten Rogers and Ashley Greene.'

She sat up and looked down at him, Julius lying with his elbows out, his hands behind his head.

'Do you think I'm two people Julius?'

'I think your profession inhibits you.'

'I'm on show, cameras flashing at me.'

'You're desired, but what do you feel when you feel desire?'

'Afraid.'

She watched him in his sleep, unperturbed by the things that troubled most men. She watched him shower the following morning and held back just how good she thought he was, not used to feeling this way. And yet he remained a mystery over breakfast. He seemed to know all about her and he'd told her next to nothing about himself. She sliced into her grapefruit as Julius buttered his toast, and she looked at the glow on his face, and his eyes that were on fire with a dangerous sexual knowledge, and it was almost as if he was female in his knowing of a woman's mind and body, but yet he was a man, there was no doubt about that.

She'd slept with women and found a lot of the things missing from her encounters with men, but with Julius there was nothing missing at all, he gave her what she craved. It was her craving he'd discovered. And as she looked at him she thought he was a whore. The best looking whore she'd ever seen.

11

Tammy had waited for the call after she got the earlobes. But it didn't come. They were her earrings. He'd placed them tidily in the box, like a jeweller would. There was this sense of precision and butchery about The Pimp's grim offerings, a juxtaposition inducing nausea. That morning Tammy tried to calculate when and how he'd managed to steal them, thinking back to the last time she'd worn them, maybe a week ago. She thought through all the recent events and of how The Pimp could be watching her without her getting a sighting of him. Her feet were feeling a lot better and she went for a walk round the block that morning, looking for men sitting in parked cars, but she saw none.

She went to the office and worked on another case, that of a killer who called himself The Beekeeper. He'd been picking women up on motorways, and deserted country roads. They'd all broken down with a puncture and needed a tyre change. But his interest in tyres went beyond the merely mechanical. The Beekeeper coated his victims' bodies in latex, and he made them dance as he took pictures of them. He sent a picture of each victim to the police. Tammy found the parallels between his murders and The Pimp's interesting. Both men were obsessed with mouths. While The Pimp removed his victims' lips and saved body parts, The Beekeeper got his victims to stand inside a tyre before he coated their mouths with honey and filled them with bees. He'd killed two women in the early part of the year and now had gone quiet. It had been some months since there had been any activity from him. Meanwhile The Pimp had increased his. It felt to Tammy as though he'd placed her under constant surveillance. As she read through her notes on The Beekeeper her mind was elsewhere, on her sister and the body parts The Pimp collected the way some men garner weapons. And in a sense that was what they were, ways of injuring her further than she already was, a means of inflicting a vivid understanding of Holly's mutilation and murder.

She returned home late that afternoon. She thought of what Joyce had said about The Pimp, of how she said he stains you. And Tammy realised that he used the past to injure. He was giving her Holly piece by piece and in doing so immersing her in what her sister went through, forcing her to live in the events that formed the final days of her life, making the torture and the violation more and more real. The fact that he'd watched her take a bath made her feel like washing. The brief sense of privacy the debugging company afforded her had already been erased by the latest gift from The Pimp, and she found herself drawing the curtains and opening a bottle of Merlot before going to bed early. She was startled by the phone ringing next to her head at 1:00 AM.

'Bet you like the touch, entering her skin with your cheap little hooks. Do you like glass, can't afford jewels, the real thing?'

'I'm having you watched, surveillance runs two ways,' Tammy said, sitting up in bed.

'This is where you try to turn the tables, that's right. You'll have to do better than that to get into my head and guess what happens next.'

'I know what happens next, I kill you and you're forgotten.'

'That vibrator you use, your only companion, does it know what a frustrated little dike you are?'

'You think I wanted my sister sexually because you're sick beyond repair.'

'I know you wanted her, Tammy, you can have her, all of her, piece by piece.'

'I'm going to find you, you know that.'

'No you won't, how are your feet?'

'The glass didn't hurt.'

'I bet you wanted to catch that paper boy, I saw you limp out into your tidy front garden and dart glances up and down the empty street, except it wasn't empty, I was there watching you, but you couldn't see me because you're not good at this game. I paid him, of course I did. But any attempt by you to get a description or location is pointless. I disguised myself, all he knows is a man asked to put something in your newspaper. You see, you'll never catch me. But you will be my whore.'

'I have a good description of you, Joyce gave it to me.'

'She's a lying whore.'

He hung up and Tammy got out of bed for some water. As she crossed the room she stumbled on something cold and hard and turned on the light. Lying on the floor was a Remington rifle pointing at her buzzer. She glanced out into the hall, but she knew he wasn't there, knew he was saying he could come and go any time he liked. He must have watched her sleeping as he moved the buzzer and placed the rifle next to it. A sense of invasion crawled across her skin and she felt cold.

She went downstairs and inspected all the rooms, finding the house as she had left it. No sign of his entry. She got a glass of water. Then she put on her latex gloves, went back upstairs and inspected the weapon. It looked new and she opened it to see if it was loaded. But instead of bullets in the chamber were pieces of rolled up paper.

They were pictures of Holly naked and with her hands tied behind her back. In one of them a knife was pointing at her breasts, its tip inches from her nipples.

12

Karen was getting ready to go out when Micky came in with a small case. He stood in the doorway of their bedroom, watching as she put on some makeup. Their glances seemed to be so frequently exchanged in mirrors it was if is she was living two lives, the one she'd married into and the other one, the life Micky kept hidden from her and which she feared. She paused, not wanting to turn round and face him, looking at him in the narrow frame, as if it was rendering his movements static, converting his threat into a piece of history, like a portrait of an ancestor with a violent past, whose deeds could no longer cause harm. As she looked at him it was as if two men occupied his body, and the man she married was becoming diminished by the day, as if a parasite had worked its way into his mind and was devouring him, leaving something she abhorred and hated in its place. But the mirror did not freeze him, nor did its frame prevent his penetration of her tattered dignity. Micky came into the room and stood inches behind her, then laid his hot palm on the back of her neck.

'It's time.'

'No, not again, I won't do it again.'

'It is your compulsion. You are my wife.'

'No Micky.'

He led her to the bed. Karen closed her eyes. It wasn't sex he wanted, that was bad enough. But this other thing was inexpressible. Karen said it in her mind, said the two words that were empty of meaning now, self-respect. Micky had eroded their sense and left her with the empty promise of the time when this would end, his use of her for the fever of his disease. For that is what it was like, an illness that reached a point at which he relaxed for a few weeks, became bearable, human again, this man she dreaded touching her. Once upon a time Micky had use his hands like a lover would, now they were those of a sexual torturer, a corrupter of the feminine. Her friends had become fewer over the years, their inability to understand why she didn't leave him an irritant to the wound she carried about like a poisoned memory of who she once had been. He'd taken her away and Julius had brought her back that night on his sheets. She didn't exist, except between the two extremes of Micky's annihilation of her dignity and Julius's renewal of her womanhood. He did it with his hands and his tongue, but so did Micky. For every violation her husband inflicted in her Julius could give her the erotic high she'd felt that night. As Micky removed his shirt and opened her eyes, one by one, gently, with the tips of his fingers, Karen almost screamed at the thought of not seeing Julius again. That would leave her with nothing. She felt as though she was falling into the crack between the two lives, the one of constant debasement and the barely born other life, the one she tried to picture with Julius, who now seemed as remote and tenuous as the refrain of a song that was fading from her mind.

Micky was unbuttoning his shirt. The cuts had scarcely healed from the last time, and she averted her gaze from the scars. He paused, shirt in hand and then threw it on the bed. She knew what would happen next, she knew every instance of this sadomasochistic pantomime she inhabited as a sexual prisoner. Micky went into the bathroom and came back with the knife he kept on the edge of the bidet. He rubbed the handle and then handed it to her.

'I don't want to cut you,' she said.

'You do.'

'What does it do for you?'

'Rids me of it.'

'Of what?'

'The need to break every bone in your face.'

'Where do you go to on your trips Micky?'

'Are you going to use that on me or am I going to have to cut your flesh?'

She looked away as she did, running the blade down his chest until a two inch gash showed on his skin and the blood beaded and dripped from it like tears. She tried to think of beautiful things but they were displaced from her. And Micky put his finger in his wound and tasted it, a serene look on his face, like a little boy again, she thought, that little boy who'd gone through all those things, the things he told her when they first met. She'd felt so much for him when they were younger, all those years ago. She never thought he'd been lying, not for one minute. And even now she wasn't sure.

'That's love,' Micky said.

'Scars and bleeding, that's all you know.'

Karen shook her head. The scars ran across his skin like tiny worms, and one cicatrix looked just like a fish hook.

'You did it to stop me from using it on you,' Micky said, 'that's love.'

'No it's not, it's the madhouse of your pleasure.'

'What do you think pleasure is Karen?'

'Not this, remember all those years ago making love to me in a summer garden, the smell of roses in my hair?' Karen said.

She touched his face, briefly recalling how pleasure felt.

'Take your filthy hands off me,' Micky said.

'There's nothing filthy about me.'

'You need to take a bath.'

'I've taken a bath.'

'Use a brush with hard bristles.'

'It cuts my skin.'

'It's what a scrubber needs.'

'I am not a scrubber.'

Micky put his right hand inside his mouth as if he was fishing for the root of his tongue. His eyes bulged, he forced his fingers in to the wrist. He began to choke. When he pulled it out spittle hung from his chin. He looked at his palms, damp with saliva and pink from the blood on his chest.

'That's what it feels like, inside you, gums without teeth, Karen.'

'I'm not washing for you, not today, hit me if you want to.'

Micky went into the bathroom and returned with several plasters that he began to stick on his skin. Then he got a fresh shirt from the cupboard.

'I'm going on a trip, Karen,' he said.

'You know they told me about it.'

'About what?'

'What you did, I don't think you meant to kill that boy.'

'I didn't kill anyone, what are you talking about?'

'Is that why you do it?'

'Do what?'

'Put your hand down your mouth when you're in pain.'

'I do not, are you having a joke with me?'

'You forced him to eat bees, Micky, he died of shock, and you tried to get them out of his mouth, but you were a little boy, you didn't know.'

'Who told you this rubbish?'

'Your sister.'

'She's winding you up.'

'You were visiting a friend, and his sister got you to touch her, privately, you know, you got angry with your friend because he watched you, and you were frightened of his sister, she was a lot older. You took him to the beehive at the end of the garden. You had gloves on, and you put them in his mouth. Has it never occurred to you why you don't wear gloves ever? Because you think it made you a coward.'

'I've never heard such bollocks.'

'Mouths and fannies feel just the same to me, you used to say.'

'I'm going to be late.'

'You never keep honey in the house.'

'I prefer jam Karen, as you know, thick red raspberry jam with seeds in it, hundreds of little seeds like the ones that clog up your menses.'

He went downstairs and she heard the door slam, then his Bentley started up on the drive. She stood by the window and watched it disappear and the gates close. She got her handbag from the chair in the bedroom and removed her mobile phone. Then she called Micky.

'That wasn't nice what you said.'

'What did I say Karen?'

'About menses.'

'You know how thick I am, what does that mean, is it a type of prostitute?'

'The fact that I can't have kids.'

'Can't you have kids?'

'Stop using it to hurt me.'

'And you who just cut my skin.'

'What sort of life would they have with you as a father anyway?'

'Do you want me to turn this car around, and come back there and break your teeth?'

'How long will you be gone?'

'Till Friday.'

She hung and went to check that the tracking device she'd placed in his car the night before was working. It was no larger than a USB stick and she'd placed it in the glove box while Micky showered. Now she watched his route on her laptop, making sure he was leaving the area. She'd begun to fear he was going to trick her by saying he was going away and returning unexpectedly.

Micky left Sheen and travelled to the A4, then got on to the M4 and went out of London. That was when she called Julius.

'It's Karen, are you free tonight?'

'Of course, what time?'

She arranged to meet him at 7:00 PM at his flat. She had some lunch at home, enjoying a glass of Pinot Grigio, and checked Micky's route again. He was still driving, over a hundred miles away, and she felt an exhilaration as she went upstairs to get ready. She washed Micky off her skin, letting the hot water course down her body, thinking of the night ahead, then she put on her sexiest underwear and a new dress she picked out a few days before, long, black, classy. She slipped into some matching heels, packed an overnight bag and drove to Kew in her blue Honda Civic Sport, feeling aroused and craving Julius.

13

He was wearing a pearl white shirt, unbuttoned at the top, showing his tanned, muscled chest, and a pair of black trousers, and he looked so good standing there. He let her in and they had some wine, but all Karen wanted was him inside her again. She kept thinking of how little time she had until Micky returned.

'How's it been with your husband?' Julius said.

'It feels like rape when he touches me.'

'Karen, that's no good. You really think he's a killer?'

'He's doing something violent.'

'Who do you think he's killing?'

'Women, Julius.'

'Why?'

'I think he hates them, I think he hates me. I feel it when he has sex with me.'

'Men like him usually kill over business. Why would a wealthy man risk everything?'

'Because there's something he's hidden from me all through our marriage.'

'What?'

'I found blood, I also found a piece of torn picture, it was of a face, a bruised face.'

Julius sipped his wine and she wondered if she'd said too much, maybe he'd think she was crazy. After all, all he knew of her was what she showed him in bed. Suddenly Karen wanted to unburden herself of her past and her marriage. She wanted to tell Julius things that would show him she wasn't imagining it, she wanted him to take her away from Micky. Or did she want him to take Micky away she wondered. She didn't want her husband's hands on her body any more.

'This picture,' Julius said.

'I think it's someone he hurt, I think he takes shots because they turn him on.'

'Was it male or female?'

'I couldn't see, it was a fragment in his pocket.'

14

It was as it had been before, rich, sensual, and he gave her every thrill she wanted and more. She drifted into his touch as he slowly removed her dress, then her bra and panties, sliding them down her legs and touching her there in the bedroom with only the sound of the distant hum of traffic outside. He did it all to her, stepped straight from her inner desires and she came twice, long and hard.

She took him in her mouth and tasted his manhood, feeling younger by ten years, her marriage absent from her thoughts as she explored his body. Julius entered her again and she took him deep inside her, high on the last orgasm, wanting another one. And she got them, one after the other like a series of fireworks exploding inside her, taking her to the limits of pleasure. But her reality became tenuous within the pleasure, as if she was immersed in a fantasy from which she could not disengage herself. The things that Julius did to her were part of her sexual dreams, the ones she'd used to sustain herself all these years, he'd entered her private world without even knowing who she was, and she wondered lying there, how he knew her hidden places.

She thought it was his touch that was so different to other men's, then she thought it was the way he went about it. But she couldn't define the precise ingredient he had that she'd never known before in other men. She'd had a few before Micky came along. But no one like Julius, no one who even came close.

And she began to fear the loss of it. As she touched him, savouring him, Karen suddenly understood addiction. She knew what it was, the compulsion to need more and more of something. He was giving her something more than arousal. It felt like a sin, as if he'd ushered her into a world of sexual mysteries, like an erotic priest dressed in designer clothes. They got up and drank wine in the living room, Karen wearing his shirt, nothing underneath it, Julius in his black trousers. And she realised as she stood there taking him in, that he removed the past from her troubled mind when he made love to her.

'There's some salad and salmon in the fridge if you don't want to go out,' Julius said.

'We have it all here.'

'You hungry? I can lay the table.'

'You can lay me a hundred times and I'd never tire of your touch.'

She felt ravenous and alone as she looked at him, as if he was beyond her when he wasn't making love to her. She thought that if Micky was gone she wouldn't feel that way. And she wondered if she was lying to herself, and if desire made her need to lie, but Karen knew that all she wanted was Julius. They sat in the kitchen and ate, but the food did not allay the famine in her bruised heart.

15

Tammy spent the morning looking through the CCTV footage taken at her house and her new office. There was nothing there. She'd spent a lot of money on the best surveillance equipment including tracking devices for emails and phone calls. And yet The Pimp evaded all her efforts at detection. That afternoon she got a lead from his last phone call. All the way to a basement in Fulham.

It was a rundown part of the otherwise affluent area, a neglected road near to prohibitively priced houses and trendy shops and bars. As she parked Tammy felt she was in the older part of Fulham, the part that had failed to shed its tatty past. The house from which he made the last call, according to her tracking information, was a peeling Victorian building that had been converted into flats. But neither the landlord nor the owners cared for their dwelling, as the worn and faded facade clearly showed. Tammy descended the crumbling steps to a rotting door. As she looked at the lock she saw that someone had removed the mechanism. She could see through the chipped and rotten wood into the hallway. For a moment she hesitated. He'd never given any details of his whereabouts away, and was this instance deliberate? Was she about to step into a trap? Tammy glanced around her, at the littered steps, and the pavement above it. Then she drew her Glock, pushed the door open and entered a dank hallway.

There were two doors off it and she opened the first one, holding her gun in front of her, scanning the room. But it was empty save only for the pictures on the walls.

The light was on so she could see them. And she knew she was in The Pimp's territory. The walls were covered with naked pictures of Holly. Holly on stage, dancing before a crowd, Holly in a cold room with concrete walls, a spotlight shining on her breasts, Holly screaming, Holly being cut with the knife Tammy recognised from the other photos. The Pimp was etching her sister's final moments into her mind. He must have had Holly under surveillance for some time before he abducted her, she thought.

She turned away, walked down the hallway to the other door and opened it slowly. This room was dark and she fumbled for the switch. There beneath a bare bulb hanging from a rope was a naked woman. Her wrists were tethered and the rope was looped through a beam that ran the width of the room. Her arms were fully stretched, her ribs were showing, and her head was slumped. She had cuts across her breasts and something covering her face. As Tammy approached her she saw what it was, a picture of Holly had been stapled to her cheeks. But she was alive, she was moving, trying to free her hands. Tammy spun round and checked the hallway, then she pulled a knife from her belt and cut the ropes from the woman's wrists. The woman tore the mask off.

'Get me out of here,' she said.

'Arlene, I thought you'd disappeared.'

16

Arlene's face had two gashes in it from the staples. The Pimp had left her clothes on the floor. Tammy held a tissue to her cuts, then she picked up her jeans and T-shirt, panties and bra and waited as Arlene dressed. Underneath the clothes was a brown envelope with the words, 'Tammy's porn,' written on it. Tammy guessed it contained more pictures of Holly. She didn't feel like seeing them. That was the way he worked, overwhelming you with vile sensory impressions, invading your mind like a virus. She stuffed the envelope in her coat pocket and drove Arlene to her house. She had taken a medical course in the army and she had a kit at home with which she tended to Arlene's injuries. The cuts on her breasts were superficial, but two on her face needed stitches. After she had put them in she made her a coffee and a cheese sandwich. She added two shots of whisky to the coffee and poured herself a double. She watched Arlene cradle the warm cup in her hands. It had been a month since she'd heard from her, this ex-girlfriend of Holly's.

'Did you see him?' Tammy said.

'No.'

'This guy doesn't leave women alive. How long had he held you?'

'What day is it today?'

'Thursday.'

'Then only a few days.'

'But I lost touch with you weeks ago, when you left the office.'

'I was finding it hard, you know, you and me, especially since you're Holly's sister.'

'He knows about your relationship with Holly, that's why he abducted you.'

Arlene put her cup down.

'He raped me for hours.'

'Then we've got DNA on him, don't wash,' Tammy said.

'Not with his penis, but with Holly's red stilettoes, the ones she used to dance in.'

'He's trying to kill everyone who knew her, but first he's killing our memories.'

'He didn't kill me.'

'No.'

'You know why she wore stilettoes when she stripped, because she hated them, she only wore clothes she despised for the creepoids as she called them, the men in the crowd.'

'I bet he was one of them.'

'His voice is like metal.'

'I know, I've had the calls.'

'He took me to that other room first and left me with the pictures.'

'He'd been spying on her, he's spying on me.'

'How did you find me?'

'I traced his call.'

'He wanted you to.'

'He's kept her clothes.'

'He told me about her and what he did to her as he penetrated me.'

'What did he say?'

'He said he used the blade of a knife on her, that she was so scarred by the time he'd finished she looked like butcher's meat. He said she pleaded. Did you know she was pregnant? I don't know whether to believe him or not. He says he has the foetus and he's saving it for you. He mentioned you, calling you the second whore. He said you had sex with Holly and that you and I should get back together again.'

'What happened between us was a mistake, our grief for her.'

'Is that what you feel?' Arlene said.

Arlene looked Tammy in the eyes. She was a beautiful woman, with long blonde hair and an oval face. Tammy looked at her mouth, her full lips, and her clear complexion. Even now she looked great. But as she thought of what they'd done before she disappeared she wondered if she was losing herself, and if her desire for her was about Holly. She thought about recent boyfriends and the dissatisfaction she felt in bed with them. And she asked herself if she desired other women or her grief had altered her sexually.

'I don't know what I feel,' Tammy said, 'I feel he's orchestrating all this, us, my mind, I want to kill him.'

'Can I stay here?'

'Of course.'

'I don't think what we did was about our grief for Holly.'

'I'm confused, Arlene, there used to be men in my life.'

'And now there is only one.'

'The Pimp.'

'That's why he uses that name, he owns women.'

'Can you take me through what happened when he abducted you?'

'OK.' Arlene paused, her eyes on the floor, the uneaten sandwich in front of her, the coffee getting cold. 'I was leaving a club, I remember walking to the bus stop and then nothing until the room with the pictures of Holly in it. I think he grabbed me. I was groggy when I came to, he must have put something over my mouth.'

'Chloroform.'

'Yes. Then he took me to the other room.'

'You didn't see his face,' Tammy said.

'No, he wore a mask, a leather mask.'

Arlene picked up the cup and sipped the coffee as Tammy remembered the envelope. She got it out of her coat and opened it. Inside was a small turquoise pocket book that Tammy recognised as belonging to Holly. It had the words, 'Love Letters to the man who made me come,' on it in Holly's hand.

'What is it?' Arlene asked.

'He left this under your clothes, it's something Holly has written.'

She opened it and looked at the first page.

'My thoughts are blue when I think of men, but there was only one man who ever did it for me. Then he left me with heartache and women. I strip for men now, never touching them, never wanting to. I sometimes wonder if I'll see him in the crowd, but he'd never go to a show. He wouldn't need to. I see this other man at the back, watching me.'

'These are letters Holly wrote and never sent, letters to a man she was seeing,' Tammy said.

'Holly didn't see men, you know that.'

'Not according to this. It is her hand.'

'Yes, it looks like it,' Arlene said, peering over her shoulder.

Tammy leafed through the letters. There were no dates on them, The Pimp had cut them out. Each page had that piece missing. Tammy turned to the first letter.

'I don't know how he knows me so well, but he's turned me inside out with his love. I thought I only went for women, but now I'm not sure. Or am I a liar? Do I hate men? I have dated men before, when I was younger and I always wanted a woman in my bed after they had left, and I wanted to wash them from my skin. I know my sister feels some of what I do and when I talk to her about it I see she is repressing it, her need for women. But this guy is different. I think he has some gift or if there is such a thing as a sexual drug he has it running through his veins like erotic cocaine. I want him so badly it makes me angry. And each time I go to bed with him he does something different, things no man or woman has ever done to me. He makes me high and when I am alone I need it, I need to feel what it is he does to me. His touch is like nothing I have ever experienced before. He has some ability to enter my heart and body. I love what he does with jewellery. That's why I call him Jules, my Caesar.'

'Does this mean anything to you?' Tammy said.

'Holly used to say there had only ever been one man who made her feel aroused.'

'Who?'

'A guy called Julius.'

17

7:00 PM.

Dr Marjorie Tram was visiting her sister in the countryside. She'd decided to take a short break and was driving down a country road outside Surrey when she felt the tyre go. She got out and opened her boot and discovered the jack was missing. She couldn't get a signal on her mobile and so she began to walk along the road looking for sufficient bars on her phone to call the breakdown service. That was when the white van slowed and the driver rolled down his window.

'You shouldn't walk about out here,' the driver said, 'you've heard of The Beekeeper, one woman was snatched from this stretch by him, so they say.'

'Then I'm lucky you came along,' Dr Tram said.

'You have a flat I take it? I know a garage nearby can get you fixed in no time.'

'Yes and the jack's missing.'

'Hop in.'

He opened the passenger door and Dr Tram climbed into the van.

'It's not every day you break down and a patient comes to your rescue.'

'You're a great doctor, I'd rescue you any day,' he said and winked at her.

She checked her face in the mirror on the visor as he drove away.

'How have you been? I haven't seen you in my surgery for a while,' she said.

'Busy, I've started up a new business, you could say. I'm much better, that little problem you helped me with has all cleared up now.'

'Good. Thank you for this, I've read about The Beekeeper in the papers, the idea I was in his patch made me shudder just now.'

'No shuddering in my van Dr Tram.'

'So what's the new business?' she said.

'Honey,' he said, reaching down into the pocket on the panel on his door.

Then he clamped a chloroform coated cloth over her mouth.

18

7:45 PM.

That Thursday Karen forgot about Micky, for a while. Julius made love to her throughout the slow, long, erotic afternoon.

'I keep trying to figure you out,' Karen said as they lay in bed. 'And I think I know what it is you have that's different from other men, it's a form of sexual sincerity.'

'I give you pleasure, but to touch a woman to the heart you have to touch her sexual mind.'

'You knew what I wanted from the first time we went to bed, Julius. Having sex with you is dangerous.'

'Don't you find that dangerous situations excite?'

'Micky is dangerous, he frightens me, it's his violence. You excite me, you exist in some erotic mystery, whereas most people try to convince themselves their lives are all right.'

'Do you think people are insincere?'

'I think my husband is lying to me and to himself.'

'What is it you think he is being dishonest about?'

'I sometimes think he's insane.'

'And when you married him?'

'He was someone else, not the man he has become. He's a sexual torturer.'

They went out to eat at an Italian restaurant nearby and she tried to understand what it was she still craved after hours of sex with this man who did it all so right. His lovemaking had the perfect ease of a fantasy or a dream, and it was as if she was directing him to do the things he did, all the things she wanted. But she wasn't directing him, and so he was reading her, and that was why it left her with a hunger, since it realised her fantasies and bore an air of unreality. It was as they left and walked back to his flat that she knew what she craved. It was seeing other couples returning home to lives they shared that she understood that she would always feel an emptiness that existed like a sexual ache within her until she and he were able to be a couple. Back in Julius's living room she said it, shocking herself a little as she did.

'I want to get rid of my husband.'

She realised what it sounded like and wondered if that's what she meant. She was about to explain herself when she stopped, waiting for his response.

'How will you do that?' Julius said.

'He won't give me a divorce. It's not going to be easy.'

'A trapped woman always strays.'

'I bet you've seen a few of them.'

'Do you think he knows?'

'About us? I doubt it, I haven't given him any clues and I don't intend to.'

'So how are you going to leave him Karen?'

'Do you know what the biggest turn on I had in weeks before you was?'

'Well it certainly wasn't Micky,' Julius said.

'It was thinking about him gone.'

'Gone.'

'Right.'

'And how are you going to get rid of your dangerous husband?'

'How about it Julius?'

'What are you saying Karen?'

'Let's run away together.'

'He'd find us, then what?'

'I can only think of one other way.'

'I don't think Micky's going to give you up, a man like him doesn't like to lose.'

'What if I find out what he's up to?'

'You mean in this double life he leads?'

'What if I get evidence of what he's doing, then take it to the police?'

'If you're right you'd get him put away.'

'Then that's what I'm going to do.'

'And what if he isn't a killer?'

'He's doing something that he's hiding from me.'

'What if it is another woman?'

'Then I can go for divorce.'

'He won't give it to you.'

'Do you want to be with me?'

'Yes, Karen.'

'You keep saying Micky won't let me go. It's like you want to see obstacles.'

'I've seen this thing before. I've seen many women trapped by men like him.'

'You do this for a living?'

'No.'

'I think Micky is hiding something.'

'How are you going to find out what it is?'

'Hire someone.'

'Have you thought about what he'll do if he is a killer?'

'I'm going to hire someone really good.'

'They better be, I don't want to see you hurt.'

'Let's go to bed.'

They did, and she forgot it all while he was inside her. She found so many pleasures with Julius that day that she was on a constant high. She didn't want to return to the expensive house in Sheen and wait for Micky to come home. But the idea he might find out about her nagged at her.

They were drinking wine in the living room when she asked him.

'If I do leave Micky do we have something?' she said.

'We have something now Karen, what you are talking about is being a couple.'

'That's what I want. But I feel you avoid it when I bring it up.'

'I want it, I just know it's going to be difficult.'

'Next week I'm going to have him followed.'

'If you're right about him you may be implicated.'

'If he is killing people? I can prove my innocence.'

'You hire a detective, do you tell him what you suspect?'

'I see no other way.'

'They may not take it on.'

'I've already put a tracking device in his Bentley.'

'Isn't that a risk?'

'He won't find it.'

'What has it told you?'

'He's gone out of London.'

'I suppose you could give the locations to the detective, see what they come up with.'

'Julius I imagine you see other women when you're not with me.'

'Does it matter to you?'

'Of course it matters, but if we were together it would have to stop.'

'It would.'

'I have to go.'

'He'll have another business trip soon, ring me.'

'I'll ring you before then.'

'Make sure you hire the best.'

'I already have someone in mind who I read about in the newspapers.'

She got dressed, feeling alone again, then she drove back to Sheen so she'd be there the next morning if Micky returned first thing. And she wondered what Julius did when she was away from him, claiming a little bit more of his life in her mind. She felt foolish then. She parked her car on the drive and watched the gates close then she entered the empty house.

19

11:00 PM.

Dr Tram had no recollection of what took place after her patient put the cloth over her mouth and forced her back into the seat. She did not see the country lanes pass by her window, an inapposite image of rural peace beyond the windows of the van. When she came to she was tied to a chair in a room that smelt of rubber. The door opened and The Beekeeper walked in in his white suit. He was putting on some rubber gloves as he walked up to Dr Tram.

'Rubber has a high stretch ratio, I drink from the rubber tree, that is why I am like a bee, they dip into the nectar and I dip into you, you will be my flower, open petal,' he said.

'You are mentally ill, I suspected that when you came to me with your complaint.'

'I'd got stung you see. I needed the antihistamine.'

'You said was the bees are attracted to you. I thought how odd it was at the time.'

'Handling them you can tell, you know they like you, do you enjoy latex?'

'Marcus, you need help, let me go and I will ensure you are not arrested.'

'I cannot be arrested because they cannot find me. They cannot find you either, but that is another matter.'

'You will be caught, they will send you to prison, a man like you won't cope there. Let me go and I will write a report, you'll get help.'

'Dr Tram you are going to be my flower today, I will fill you with latex, until it oozes from your mouth like cream at a birthday party.'

'Why do you call yourself The Beekeeper?'

'Because I keep bees, I subsist on a diet of rubber, I copulate with rubber dolls like you, I fill you up and I make honey.'

'It was you wasn't it? Last night.'

'I saw you glance down at the street but by then it was too late.'

'I was getting ready for bed and I heard a sound, like a car door shutting. I was sure I checked the jack was in my car that afternoon.'

'It was.'

'You moved it, you followed me.'

'How do you think I catch all the pretty young women that come to me for honey?'

'Why me?'

'That second appointment I cancelled. I watched as the replacement patient went to see you. I've read all about Tammy Wayne, interfering little bitch.'

'She's trying to track The Pimp.'

'She'll never succeed, he's too good, too slick, like a pimp should be. You have to keep the whores shackled to the bed post while you're out on a shopping spree.'

'Are you working together?'

'Me and The Pimp? A little fanciful, Dr Tram.'

'But you know something about him.'

'I know what he'll do to her when he gets hold of her.'

'So you watched her leave the surgery.'

'She'd stepped on glass, I saw that. I didn't place it there, I cancelled the appointment I had and followed her. She's been looking for me too you know.'

'She tracks serial killers.'

'But I've been watching her, so has The Pimp.'

'How did you cause my tyre to burst?'

'You stopped at a garage a few miles before the puncture. While you went to pee I stuck a nail in it, I find penetrating rubber such a turn on.'

'Is that how you trapped all your victims?'

'The first one was coincidental, then it became a high, you know, a young woman alone on a country road, inhabiting the mythology of the knight on a white charger.'

'But you're no knight, and the only white thing about you is your van, and from what I could see it's filthy.'

'You like filth, I can tell what you want.'

'Do you get aroused feeling as though you are rescuing a woman?'

'No I get aroused knowing I have caught them in my hive and that their flesh will feed the bees, my bees have an unusual diet.'

'They'll find my car.'

'They won't, I'll take it to the pound, after I have turned you into my rubber doll.'

'I imagine that's it, you can't have regular sex.'

'You can taunt me all you want, you'll see how huge my manhood is when I penetrate you, I'll turn you into lollipop as I ejaculate latex and sugar inside your candy hole.'

'Tammy Wayne is onto you,' Dr Tram said. 'I know her well, she's told me about this place.'

'Bzz bzz says the bee, you cannot play your games with me.'

'I need some water.'

'You don't need water, I'm going to fill your mouth with something much better.'

'Show me your bees.'

'Time for your examination doctor, be a good girl and open your lips.'

He picked a knife up from a chipped wooden table that stood against the darkened window and began to cut her clothes from her body. They fell away in strips as Dr Tram wrestled with the ropes. When he was down to her bra and panties The Beekeeper stood back and lifted a camera from the table. He took a shot of her then he unhooked her bra and pulled her panties down to her ankles.

'I bet you get a kick out of it,' he said.

'You think I enjoy this?'

'I bet you get a kick out of examining cocks. You feel butch inspecting male genitals.'

'You're sick.'

'Dance Dr Tram, I will untie you and you can strut your stuff for the boys.'

He sliced the ropes from her legs and hands and she lunged at him, but The Beekeeper dodged, stepping back and holding the knife out if front of him.

'I can cut you if you want but a dance will get you some dessert.'

'I'm not dancing for you.'

'Then you will have the hive.'

He removed his hat then his gloves and laid them on the table neatly. Then he walked up to Dr Tram and took her neck in his left hand and opened her lips with his right as she tried to kick him. But The Beekeeper pushed her against the wall and forced his fingers down to the back of her throat until she began to retch.

'All improbable acts of penetration will now occur at the hotel,' he said.

She buckled over and watched the saliva run down her chin as he left the room, taking the knife with him. She heard the lock turn and she walked over to the window and gazed down at a car park. His white van was parked there and the ground was covered in debris. She was about to lift the chair to break the glass when he returned.

'The glass is shatter proof,' he said.

He had a rubber tyre in one hand and what looked like an earthenware drinking vessel in the other, but as he set it down on the table she saw that it was shaped like a beehive.

'That's the shape a natural hive has,' he said.

The lips were slopping with a white liquid that gave off the intense smell of latex.

'You have a sexual fixation with rubber,' Dr Tram said.

'You're such a drone, you'd never be a Queen.'

'What did the Queen do to you? Dominate you when you were a teenager?'

'All those young girls, those adolescent whores, they drink come to keep their lips moist.'

'Why are you so obsessed with bees?'

'Because they know all about nectar.'

He put the tyre on the floor and grabbed her face with one hand. Then he lifted the hive from the table and poured the latex into her mouth until it was dripping from her chin.

'Step into the tyre,' he said.

She tried to scratch his face but he grabbed her hands and lifted her into it. He rubbed the latex all over her face and breasts as it began to harden. Then he removed a condom from his pocket. He tore the wrapper and pulled at it, tugging on the end and lengthening it as he stretched it.

'Why don't you have sex with me?' Dr Tram said.

'You sly thing, trying to get me on the floor so you can run away.'

He placed the condom over her head and Dr Tram began to gasp. She could see the milky white shape of The Beekeeper as he donned his suit and hat. Then he opened the door and left the room and she heard them swarming in. He came back in with a jar of honey in his hand and he rubbed it all over her body as the bees began to feed.

20

Friday 12:00 AM.

When she got back Karen checked her laptop for Micky's whereabouts. But the tracking device had lost him. Micky had left London and then there was no information. Karen wondered whether she had bought a defective device or he had found it and was now heading home. She drank a glass of cognac, feeling its warmth work its way into her belly and erase her fear a little. Then she fed the dogs at the back of the house. The cleaner had come and gone while she'd been with Julius. Karen had left a note saying she had some shopping errands and asking her to feed them. The strips of sirloin steak Micky kept for them reminded her of flesh, torn and tattered, grey in the moonlight that made the dogs' eyes look like they were shot full of silver.

She went to bed and thought of Julius making love to her. She was woken in the early hours of the morning by Micky coming into the bedroom. She put the light on and looked at him, standing there staring down at her, his expression angry. Micky began to undress. Then he pulled the sheets back. Karen was wearing a nightie and he lifted it up, but she took hold of his hand and stopped him.

Micky squeezed her hand, Karen struck out at his face, but he grabbed her other wrist. He bent over and peered at her, his mouth as tight as if it had been stitched shut, a smell like cordite on his clothes. He said nothing and his eyes reminded her of the dogs', his thoughts unreadable, as unreachable as a canine's.

'Micky stop,' Karen said.

'You think I want a shag.'

'You'll have to wait. You can't just come in here like this.'

'I can.'

'These business trips of yours.'

'They make me want you.'

'I think you're seeing another woman.'

'There is no other woman.'

He let her go and began to undress, his movements slow and measured. Then he peeled away the plaster from the cut she'd administered before he left. The skin had gone blue. He lay down next to her and he turned on the mattress and brought his face to within inches of hers.

'I want to tattoo your face,' he said.

'I don't want a tattoo Micky.'

'I've got one, look.'

'I'm tired.'

He got onto his knees and straddled her and pointed at the cut. The words, 'My wife likes to cut me,' ran across it in blue ink.

He turned over and went to sleep. Karen lay in the dark with her back to him, and she thought of how she would get away from him. She saw the chains that shackled the dogs to the house. She saw them in moonlight, running across her body link by link. She woke before him the follow morning and made some coffee. His attaché case was on the kitchen table and she went through it looking for clues, finding none. When Micky came down he stood in front of her as she sat in the kitchen eating breakfast and he unzipped his fly.

'I need to go shopping,' Karen said.

'You know what I got in here.'

'I know what you got in there.'

'I don't mean my cock. Something else.'

'What then?'

'Something I found in my Bentley.'

'Look I don't know what this is all about.'

'I want to show it to you.'

'Show it to me.'

'I found a tracking device.'

21

Holly's letters made interesting reading. Tammy and Arlene had pored over them, this record of Holly's private world bringing them closer, both physically and emotionally. They sat side by side on the sofa, reading and re-reading what she'd written. There were pages and pages about Julius, about how he was in bed. Holly had tried to define what it was he had, as if she needed to identify some sexual ingredient in order to rid herself of a man in her life. In one entry she'd written, 'I'm a lesbian and what he does to me is denaturing me, piece by piece. He is making me doubt who I am.'

There were reflections on sex, on how she viewed men and her observations on Julius. The last entry in the book read, 'He has an ability to make me feel something I have never known, something so strange and erotic it scares me. When he makes me come I feel high for days, I can feel his fingers inside me when am not with him, and I crave him all the time. I followed him today and saw him with another woman. And I found out what it is he is hiding, I have thought so many things, that maybe he swings both ways, that he is a gigolo, that he is married, I knew he had a secret life, but what I discovered is more-.'

It ended there with a tear in the page. Behind it, at the back of the book was a note from The Pimp. 'Bet you want to read the rest, hah? How this guy got the hook into Holly's heart. Maybe he was hung like a horse, think about that Tammy as you handle your Glock. You'll have to wait and find out, special delivery.'

That morning it came. Tammy was chewing a piece of toast when she opened the front door for the postman and saw a box lying on her mat. It had been hand delivered. She took it into the kitchen and opened it carefully, ignoring her mail. It was wrapped in tissue paper and inside it were two sets of eyelashes. They looked fake but Tammy knew all too well that The Pimp liked to send body parts. Beneath them were the typed words, 'She killed them with her eyes, but he got her every time.'

Arlene came into the kitchen drying her hair with a white towel, as Tammy stared at the latest gift from the Pimp. Arlene was wearing a pair of faded jeans and a peasant blouse, and her feet were bare. She stared over Tammy's shoulder. The eyelashes were stuck to the bottom of the box, but there was something else in the box, something metallic.

'What is that underneath them?' Arlene said.

'I think it's a bullet.'

Tammy put on her latex gloves and carefully lifted the eyelashes out with a pair of tweezers. The lashes tore and she stopped momentarily, her sharp intake of breath unnaturally loud in the quiet room where both women felt the rapid beating of their hearts like birds' wings in their breasts, raising waves of grief. Tammy felt as though she was injuring her sister, but she continued to pull at them, knowing she had to investigate. The bullet was a .22 calibre hollow point, and there was something inside the case. Tammy lifted it out slowly. It was a piece of rolled up paper. Tammy opened it and set it on the table. On it were the words, 'disturbing than any of these things, at least to me, but it makes sense now, it all makes sense, why he is the way he is in-.'

Tammy's phone rang on the table next to her, making her and Arlene jump. Arlene put her hand to her chest as Tammy answered, knowing who the caller would be.

'Bang!' The Pimp said. 'In bed, that was what she wrote, in bed, I have the rest here but you'll have to read it when I tie you up and kill you, Tammy. Enjoy Arlene, enjoy every inch of her feverish lesbian skin, because one day it will be rags of meat. You're my whores now, and both of you can put on a show for me.'

He hung up before she had time to compose herself enough to speak. Then her CD player clicked on across the hallway in the living room and The Flaming Lips When Yer Twenty Two blasted at full volume out of the speakers. Tammy and Arlene went through and stared at the player, as the song filled the room, as if The Pimp had arranged for a band to mock them in their home. Tammy hit the remote and shut it off, then she pulled the CD out. It had a label stuck to the front with the typed words, 'I love them at that age, they still smell of teen cunt,' on it.

'He's in the house, all the time, why don't we move out?' Arlene said.

'I'm not going to be driven out of my home.'

'He has access to your world. It's like he's got us on remote control.'

'He's a hacker, that's all.'

'Can't you trace the package?'

'He delivers them by hand, or gets someone to do so.'

'That song about being twenty two.'

'The age Holly was when he killed her. And the bullet is a .22 calibre.'

Tammy went to get ready. Arlene came back to work for her that day of broken memories, that day of realising they were living under such an intensive surveillance it all seemed too hard, to catch a man who did these things. But Tammy was not going to be put off. At the office she set about dealing with emails and thinking of ways she could place The Pimp under surveillance. Arlene took calls and settled in as naturally if she had never left.

And Tammy found herself watching her a little too intently, Arlene dressed in a figure hugging black skirt and blue blouse she'd left at Tammy's house a few weeks earlier when she'd stayed the night, before she'd disappeared. Tammy wanted her, and asked herself what was wrong with that? But it was Holly she desired beneath Arlene's clothes, the trace of Holly in this woman who had been her partner. Arlene noticed Tammy was watching her and raised her eyes from her computer screen.

'You think there's a reason he left me alive,' Arlene said.

'I think he's studying us, like insects, I think he's obsessed with watching before he kills.'

'When will he try to make his move?'

'When he's got aroused enough.'

'And when will that be?'

'When he's seen enough fear in us.'

22

Karen had thought Micky knew it was her who had placed the tracking device in his Bentley. But strangely, after showing it to her he said it was a business rival. Karen stood there trying to act cool, asking who would do that. Micky said there were plenty of people who'd try to get hold of his money.

'But why track you?' Karen said.

'They want to find out where I have business investments.'

'What would that achieve? They'd have a location, that's all.'

'They want access to files.'

'You mean all the stuff you keep offline?'

'Right.'

'What are you going to do?'

'Find out who put it there.'

Karen realised she was arguing against an explanation that favoured her but she didn't believe Micky thought it was a rival, not at first. He put the tracking device down on the counter. Then he went into his office and made some calls. She could hear his voice in the hallway, trying to find out who did it. When he came out Karen was wondering if there was a way the device could be linked to her laptop. She studied his face, and thought he looked angry.

'If you find out who put the device there, what are you going to do?' she said.

'I'll deal with them.'

'Did you find anything out? Maybe you can trace where it was bought.'

'No point, besides I've got other things on my mind.'

'Like what?'

'Getting you a tattoo, a nice one on your arse.'

'I told you I don't like needles.'

'I want it to say, "I belong to Micky."'

'You know I do.'

'Do I?'

'When do I say or do anything you don't want me to?'

'When I go away.'

'I stay here and watch those dogs snarl.'

'That's what you say, Karen.'

'And it's the truth.'

'You know what I'd do, don't you, if I caught you with another fella?'

'Yeah, I know Micky.'

'Let me show you something.'

He took her upstairs to the spare room and opened the padlock on the cupboard he always kept locked. It was a cupboard full of knives tucked into leather straps.

23

Julius met Ashley again that evening. They drank wine at a bar then she took him back to her flat and undressed in the living room, taking off her sheer blouse slowly, Julius hadn't seen it under the jacket she had on, her eyes on his, giving him her sexy look, Julius liking it. Ashley thought she'd give him all her moves, the ones she used on the catwalk, the ones the magazines loved and which got the paparazzi snapping their cameras. She slipped down the violet skirt, standing there in a bright pink G-string and a black bra, cute now. She reached back and unhooked it, lowered it slowly, cupping her hands over her nipples, removed one then the other. She kicked off her heels and pulled down the G-string before going upstairs, slightly drunk, swaying a little as she moved, looking good with those tight buttocks and long tanned legs going all the way to where Julius was headed, Julius following, watching as Ashley ran a bath and got in, waiting for him to join her, one hand on the edge of the tub, her knockout eyes full of desire.

Julius undid his ivory white shirt, Ashley digging his chest, then he slipped out of his jeans, and pulled down his jockeys. Ashley reached up and cupped her hand around his cock, watched it stiffen and stir as she dipped her other hand below the water and opened her mouth, waiting.

Julius bent and kissed her, and she pulled him towards her, putting her tongue deep in his mouth. He touched her nipples, caressing them softly at first, then more firmly, hard now, feeling her full breasts. Ashley lifted her other hand out of the water, still holding Julius's cock, loving how hard it was. She put her finger in his mouth.

His indigo eyes gave nothing away, even though she tried to go beneath his gaze to what was underneath. She wanted to coax him out of his sexual composure.

'How do I taste?' she said.

'Of depravity, needful Ashley.'

'Me needful? I can get what I want.'

'Only a certain kind of man would know your hidden things.'

'And you're that guy, the one who pulled me in a bar.'

'You know I am. You know I can.'

'I am depraved, it's true, it comes with the body.'

He got in the bath, touched her and watched her neck flex, looking at the tiny blue veins that threaded across the surface of her clear skin as she became more aroused. Ashley was moaning now, the moans coming hard and fast, and Julius thought they sounded on the verge of pain. She stood up and grabbed him, flung her long arms around his neck and pulled him towards her, her back to the wall. Julius entered her knowing how she wanted it, hard, slapping her arse against the tiles.

As she came she dragged her nails across his back and stood there wanting more. They got out of the bath and towelled down then went into the bedroom. Ashley pushed Julius onto the bed, got on top of him, leaned forward and took him inside her with her hand, her other hand feeling his muscles. She rode him, moving slowly at first, looking for the pleasure in his face. Julius grabbed her buttocks and pulled her down onto his cock, reaching up and brushing her nipples with the tips of his fingers. Ashley was moving faster now, waiting for him to come and needing it.

His self-control was beginning to unnerve her and she wondered what his secret pleasures were. She searched his eyes for hunger.

Then she felt it coming and she kept the rhythm going. She joined him as he came, rich and long and hard. It left her sweating on the bed, liquid now, her skin slick with sex and pleasure. Julius was still hard and she wondered how as her ecstasy fought her fear. The thought of other women entered her mind and the room was filled with female voices saying things she couldn't hear. And she wanted to hear them, she wanted to know what he did with them all. Because he had to, he had to have a hundred women, a man like him.

Ashley was experiencing something she didn't know or understand. She'd always been in charge sexually since the age of sixteen when she bloomed into a model. She had her pick of guys and they could never match what she fantasised about in bed, so she had women, lots of chicks, but the experience left her hollow and alone and she craved man again, veering between the two pleasures.

Julius was different, she'd never met or screwed a man like him before, attentive and capable of anything she wanted. And it was how he knew what she wanted that troubled and thrilled her the most.

She wondered if she became someone else in bed whether he would adapt to it, this man who was so ready to stimulate her body in every way.

Ashley's ambivalence was instilling a sexual pain in her, she wanted Julius too much, and it made her afraid to think of what he did when she wasn't around. He was the kind of guy who could walk into any bar in the world and have any woman he wanted. And so what did they have? It began as sex, it always began as sex. But now she wanted more.

She thought she'd see where it went, as if she could erode his sexual veneer and penetrate him, discovering the kind of man who she knew how to dominate with her body. Was it a veneer she wondered. She knew how to act sexy, she did it on the catwalk. She felt threatened by his certainty, as if beneath the pleasure he provided was a sexual insult. And so she reached down and took his cock in her hand again, amazed at how hard it still was. Ashley lay back and parted her legs and pulled him towards her. And Julius entered her again, riding her hard into the night as she wondered who he was, this irresistible stranger in her bed. She formulated questions in her mind, things she would ask him later and she rejected them as she came.

They sat and drank wine, naked, and she touched him, craving his body, wanting more and feeling her desire turn into an ache. And the wine made her higher and locked into the sexual pleasure that was coursing through her body. Ashley knew Julius so well in bed. And yet she didn't know him at all.

That night she watched him as he slept, and searched his face for secrets she wanted to plunder to fill the hole that was swelling inside her. And she wondered if too much pleasure could be a bad thing. The thought had never occurred to her before, she'd always enjoyed sex and never questioned what she did in bed or with whom. And so the difference that Julius represented filled her all through the night with an insatiable hunger. It engendered thoughts of violence in her, and she imagined maiming the other women who dwelt like spectres in her head and shared with her a thing she wanted to own entirely, the language of Julius's hands.

She took his fingers and put them inside her as he lay with his eyes shut and she thought he knew, sensed it all, all those fears racing beneath her conscious mind. She was nearing it again, another orgasm, as she used him and he slept and this gave her a sense of control. And she wondered how old he was, older than her, she thought, somehow unknowable. Inasmuch as she loved his sexual prowess she wrestled with it, for it represented a fundamental moral dilemma. It was a quandary of where desire might lead her, and of the morally compromised choices she might make.

These were the thoughts that passed through Ashley's head, but vaguely, like sensations, the instincts of an animal sensing danger as she climaxed and pushed Julius's fingers deep inside her as if she wanted to eat them and all the hidden things they knew of female desire. When he woke the next morning she was making coffee in his shirt.

He came into the kitchen in his jockeys and kissed her. He ran his hand under the shirt and felt her bare skin, her breasts, parting her thighs as she lifted herself up on the counter and wrapped her legs around his waist. Ashley was back in the high again, loving it, wanting more. She came there as he screwed her and the smell of coffee and sex filled the room. It was the fact that he could do it just the way she needed it, every time, that made him seem unreal. She wanted to penetrate him, to know his mind. But he remained unreadable to her. He never said the things that other men said and he probably didn't share their thoughts. As she looked at him she thought the only way to find out about him was through sex. She needed to do something more extreme to find out where his limit lay. And then it occurred to her that maybe he didn't have one.

24

He gave her what she secretly desired. And she wondered how he knew, he seemed to sense her hidden recesses, all those places she'd lived in as a teenager admired by everyone she met, desired by too many to name. Julius had this knack of climbing inside you, she thought, and then she became more afraid that she'd ever been. If she fell for this man, if she felt love for him then he had her heart and that would never do. She wanted him back inside her, deep inside where she could gauge the level of his desire, she needed him to love her and desire her more than any other woman and as she admitted the impossibility of guaranteeing this she denied the truth to herself. What Ashley pushed away was how fragile the pleasure he gave her made her feel. It conjured the spectre of loss from erotic arousal, it brought with it fear and danger. Ashley liked danger, she enjoyed its sexual charge. And she asked herself was there nothing she wouldn't do to keep this man, knowing the answer before she finished the thought.

Ashley got dressed in her best outfit, items from a catwalk she'd done for the best designers in London and they went out to lunch that day when rain gave way to a bright sunshine. They dined nearby at Gigolo, a small Italian restaurant, a bright and polished place with couples exchanging romantic glances over table cloths on which sat small elegant carafes of imported Tuscany wine, and Ashley felt important and significant in Julius's life. She noticed the looks women gave him and how he avoided returning them when he was with her. When he was with her, that was the problem, he wasn't most of the time. And as they talked of things they would do later at her flat she tried to calculate a way to secure him for herself once and for all. She thought of the various seductions she held in her list of sexual skills, and she knew sitting there listening to him talk that she had none that could match the talents of Julius, since he knew them all and seemed able to melt into the many men she hungered for in her fantasies. He inhabited them as an erotic reality while remaining remote. She didn't like that.

Never dominated, always dominant, Ashley existed as a female predator who enjoyed leaving stains in other's hearts. Then she would leave. She remained, so she believed, eternally desired just because of this, her desertion of lovers hooked on her. She was a pusher of sexual addictions.

'There are things I can do for you in bed,' she said to Julius as she licked cream from her spoon at the end of the meal.

His eyes held hers, an intense blue light, unwavering and unreadable and she felt her desire throb beneath the chic blue skirt she was wearing. She wanted to touch herself there beneath the table and have him enter her in the clean bathroom at the back. She wanted to hear him groan inside her while others ate and returned to dull lives. And she wanted to sneer at them all, the unbeautiful men and women she saw every day. But Julius never groaned and it made her wonder why. The prospect of her own limits of appeal nagged at her as they spoke of sex and pleasures, of the deep erotic night.

'Beyond what you have already done?' Julius said.

He often took his time to answer her. Ashley liked that about him, how he seemed to savour his words and thoughts before offering them to her.

'You know with you I feel, you do it all for me, you give me so much. And I want to feel I drive you a little mad in the sack.'

'You do.'

'Do I?'

'Can't you tell when I'm inside you?'

'I can tell you're enjoying it yes, you're the best lay I've ever had, maybe ever will.'

'And?'

'And I want you, I want you all to myself, Julius.'

'Do you see anyone else around?'

'That's not what I mean.'

'You're worried I'm playing around.'

'I wonder what you do when you're not with me.'

'You don't strike me as the jealous type.'

'You see, there you go. You dodge things, cleverly.'

'Is that a dodge?'

'Julius I want you, I want us to be more than an occasional fuck.'

'How could I not share that desire?'

'I don't even know what you do.'

'I'm a photographer, glamour shoots mostly.'

'Makes sense. They must love you.'

'The models?'

'I bet you shag them all.'

'You think I'm a bit of a whore?'

'I think you're a man.'

'What if I told you I don't shag them, would you believe me?'

'No.'

'What's the point in trying to convince you?'

'There's one way you could.'

'Show me.'

She did at her flat after lunch. She stripped for him, in the living room with the curtains drawn, did it slowly, Julius sitting on the sofa watching. Then she unzipped his fly and sat on his lap. Ashley looked for what she was used to seeing in the faces of the men she slept with, a momentary sense of vertigo as they entered the pleasure zone and feared the loss of her, but it wasn't there in Julius. It wasn't that he didn't enjoy her body, it was that his mind remained secured and beyond her reach, and that troubled her in ways she'd never known before.

And she thought about the other women again, those faceless beauties he encountered at work where he caressed their skins with his zoom lens. She thought of following him, of hiring a detective and placing him under constant surveillance to discover what he did when he was away from her and she realised she would only be watching his body not his mind. For it was his mind that turned her on so much, yes he had a beautiful face and a great physique, but his thoughts were unknowable and he existed as a fantasy in flesh.

She looked at him now, naked, beneath her, able to carry on all afternoon, and the images of countless bodies mounting one another flooded her head. She lay on the floor next to the unlit fire as Julius did it to her again all afternoon as she lost Ashley, the one she'd always known, the one holding the reins. It was as if within his lovemaking was a form of deep sexual surveillance, and she felt as though he was peeling her with pleasure.

She looked into his eyes and Julius seemed to open then, and she saw the craving that she felt for him and realised he was within her reach after all as the climax flooded her, and she fell into his heart and woke in pain. And she wondered why? But what she thought she was and who she was were two different things. He dwelt in the shadows, eternally seductive jester playing the strings of her desire.

She touched him, running her hands across his chest, and holding his manhood. She took him in her mouth, deep inside, wanting to suck the last drop of semen from his cock.

Afterwards they talked and drank wine in the kitchen, Ashley wearing his shirt again, feeling comfortable in his clothes. It was a way of getting inside him, or part of him. The way he was inside her. He'd entered her, but not only physically she thought. He was within her reach, after all, she told herself, and she wanted to inhabit him with desire, desire for Ashley.

'Move in with me,' she said.

'It seems a little soon.'

'I've never seen your flat. I want to know about you Julius.'

'You can see it any time you want.'

'Do you take other women there?'

'I have.'

'And now?'

'I'm here with you.'

'You know what I'm saying.'

'It sounds as though you have the beginning of an obsession.'

'Yes I think I do. It's the effect you have on me, you make me high.'

'Is that a bad thing?'

'I want to know about you.'

'What do you want to know?'

'Were you ever married?'

'No.'

'That I believe, I mean why would you?'

'Maybe I've been waiting for the right girl.'

'You've been waiting for me. Don't say I don't do it for you.'

'I think you can tell you do.'

'You've never had kids?'

'Not that I know of.'

She pointed a finger at him.

'You haven't. Any woman who bore your child would let you know.'

'And why is that?'

'They'd never let you get away.'

'There's nothing for you to worry about.'

'Yes there is, there's plenty.'

'What we just had, isn't it enough?'

'It's enough for sex, it's more than enough.'

'But you want more.'

'I want you in more ways than one, I don't want other women around you.'

'That may be a little hard given my job.'
'I mean I don't want you having other women.'
'When do you want me to move in?'
'Now, let's go to your flat.'
'I have some things I need to do first.'
'You're not messing me around?'
'Give me a week. Then I can move in, for a while.'
'A while?'
'You might not like my habits.'
'I'll like your habits well enough.'
'Then we have nothing to worry about.'
'Are you a gigolo?'
That brought a smile to his face.
'Is that how you think of me?'
'Are you?'
'Do you see any money involved?'
'I want you to meet my friends.'
'What shall I wear?'
'Don't make fun of me.'
'I'm not.'

'Julius, you seem more than one man, you can bend to my desires like no one ever before, male or female, and I've slept with both.'

'But the women left you empty and the men hungry.'

'Right, there you go again.'

'Do you want to go upstairs?'

'That's what I mean, mind reader.'

'It's all in the body Ashley. I see it in your eyes.'

'But I want to be in your mind, Julius, the way you are in mine.'

He took her up to the bedroom and unbuttoned the shirt she was wearing and made love so softly to her she felt as though another man was there again. It was as if just as soon as she had a reading on one of his styles he invented another one, to keep her guessing, to keep her wanting more. And it was this mixture of becoming familiar with him and the distancing of himself from the familiar that made him so seductive. He kept the flame of erotic beginnings alight. He existed between extreme intimacy and erotic desertion. And she only knew him in the body.

With him living with her she would find out more. So she told herself as she yielded to the deepest orgasm she had ever known. It seemed as though it would never stop. She rode the waves of pleasure that flooded her and made her tingle. And she thought of all the pleasure he must have given to other women.

Ashley saw knives flashing in corridors. She saw herself stalking the other women in a leather outfit and killing them and riding away on a motorbike. She imagined Julius making love to her afterwards, unzipping her leathers and screwing her on the kitchen table. She could see her legs knocking cutlery and chinaware to the floor as he made love to her all day long and made her feel constantly desired. She was becoming addicted to Julius and she didn't care.

She wondered if she would kill to keep him to herself. She didn't want any other woman to have what he gave. She was hungry and high and she felt herself coming again. There was no end to the pleasure this man gave. But still he seemed unreal as she wrapped her legs around his waist and drew him into her body and her mind.

To want and go on wanting even when satisfied was an anomaly so erotic that she felt the hurt rise in her all the way to what she called her stolen mirrors. These were glimpses of painful moments with others, times when Ashley had been forced to see her motives and deeds, and which lay like broken glass beneath her thoughts. Now the shards glinted back at her with fractured images of the woman she feared herself to be. She'd ridden beauty and appeal to steal away from these thoughts, but her pleasure seemed to be leaking into them now and she held onto Julius. His body could protect her against the night, his cock would keep her fertile.

She saw a million eggs breaking in her mind and swimming on a sea of bubbles as small hands clutched for them. And she recalled the first time a boy fumbled with her in the back seat of his car as she clutched for leverage on the seat, but he was too heavy and she was falling, and he pulled aside her panties as she felt him touch her, all the way to wild desires that left her empty and alone. That was what it was like now, seeing the bubbles burst and herself diminished in her flat, where she'd had so many sexual encounters. They seemed like a silent film to her against the backdrop of Julius who made the past seem as flat and static as a picture. She'd entered the scene of some drama as he entered her again and again, and she wondered what background she was in and to what as she lay there next to him. She saw that it was growing dark outside the window and she held onto Julius as she thought of the night filled with sex, the only rhythm that mattered to her now, and recalled that time all those years ago in the back of that car with that boy's hands on her body.

'You screamed that was the night as you came,' Julius said.

'That was the night I lost my virginity.'

25

8:00 PM.

He ate honey from a silver spoon, filling his mouth with it, watching the latest body in the tyre. This was sculpture of sorts, to the man called The Beekeeper. He'd wanted to do this to the doctor many times before, on visits to her surgery as she touched his skin when examining him for imagined maladies that were merely pretexts for a physical contact that ignited the dark fantasies he inhabited. For the man who Dr Tram had called Marcus needed to be touched to begin his murderous designs on the female body. Bees to him were things of beauty, agents of sex that ushered in the need to destroy and rearrange human skin.

He sat on the chair in the room and looked at her skin. It was bright with the spots left by the stings that covered it like a patchwork of blisters. He rose from the chair and approached Dr Tram, touching her body lightly with his fingers, as if brushing away some gossamer from her ravished flesh. He fingered the stings, then he knelt in an act of insect supplication, buzzing as he did. He placed his lips around a sting, sucking.

'You see, Dr Tram, I have given you many nipples now, that is why this deed is a necessity, you understand, Dr Tram, nutrient whore. I will suck the milk from your body.'

And so he did, as he had done with the others, the women he'd trapped on country lanes and brought to his hotel of honey and tyres. He sucked and sucked until he felt the sensation that allowed him to forget a while the need to torture and maim. Then he took her body down into the room filled with tyres.

'Welcome to my museum, it is filled as you can see, with all the women who asked me to provide them with extra nipples. Now I will make you into my rubber doll.'

He began to melt a vast quantity of wax in a large vat. Then he dipped the hive into it and poured it over Dr Tram's body. He placed a wick at the top. It rose out of her head like an aerial. He watched the wax harden, leaving only her genitals uncoated. Then he stood her next to the other women he housed in his museum.

26

'You're lost in the past,' Julius said, his eyes soft, his voice gentle in the twilit room.

'You're taking me there, each time you make love to me, I can't reach your mind.'

'Is it my mind you want Ashley? Is it something else?'

'You're beyond reach, you exist in the sexual acts we perform.'

'How old were you?'

'Too young, barely a teenager. But I looked far older.'

'And when you remember it?'

Ashley sat up and looked at Julius, her eyes wandering across his face. He reached up and touched her breasts, and ran his hand down her tight brown stomach.

'The boy was clumsy. He had trouble removing my clothes. I was curious, intrigued to do it. I'd made out before but never gone all the way. His cock hurt me when he put it in.'

'There is no dignity in back seat fumblings, a girl needs to be seduced.'

'That's where you come in. And you're so good at it.'

'You're an incredibly beautiful woman. It's not hard to make love to you.'

'Is it hard to make love to some women?'

'Of course.'

'Have you tried with many of them? Do you offer yourself to lonely housewives?'

'No. I am not selling sex Ashley.'

'I'm just your type.'

'You are.'

'That's a good thing. Because this is dangerous.'

'Dangerous?'

'The kind of thrills you give me could make a girl want to kill.'

'Other women?'

'Yes, you're mine and I intend to keep you.'

She got on top of him. And although she was tired she felt so many things as she rode him to her final orgasm of that night, a deep glorious drenching of sensation that shot across her body as she looked into his eyes and waited for him to come inside her, wanting it all, all the way to the heart of her body's pleasure.

She kept him inside her as she slept and dreamed of him and her alone on a deserted beach somewhere. But as she rose from the sand she saw naked women rise from the sea with salt water dripping from their erect nipples. They swarmed towards him in a line of sexual frenzy and Ashley woke clutching the sheets and drenched in sweat. Julius touched her forehead and kissed her mouth and she melted at this man's amazing capacity to read her moods and adapt himself to them, almost as a woman who inhabited a man's body.

They rose and drank coffee in the kitchen as sunlight drifted into the room, Ashley in a pair of peach pink panties and nothing else, Julius in his jockeys. She touched him under the table, felt him stir and knew then she was hooked. She was dislocated from her sense of control and sought resolution to the compromised position she found herself in. And she began to feel that Julius was playing on her fantasy, a sexual chameleon with endless appeal.

They ate breakfast and for a brief moment she felt as though they were a couple, living together, enjoying the same habits. She knew he would go that morning and she wondered if he would return, if indeed his promise to live with her was a subtle brush off. And so she resolved to have him followed.

She watched him shower and then she got dressed, putting on a light blue skirt and matching blouse. She said good bye to him as he kissed her at the door.

He looked so handsome she felt afraid again and she fought her jealousy and its strangeness. She had never felt jealous before.

'You will move in with me?' she said.

'Of course.'

The way he said it was so easy, then everything he did seemed easy, casual and intense and sincere at the same time. And so she watched him walk away, into the sunlight clutching a piece of her heart. She thought it through, this alien gesture she was making towards a security she'd never needed before. She leafed through the phone book for a private investigator. She found one and left a message for him to call her on Monday morning.

Then she wondered what it was she would find out, and what she would feel if there was nothing Julius was hiding. She wondered how many women there were, and how he managed to juggle them. He was priapic beyond belief and she craved it all, Ashley wasn't going to share. All the other men she'd known had been hers and hers alone.

27

The private investigator called her early and arranged to meet her that afternoon at her flat. Maurice Calm was a short slightly overweight man with thick hands and small watchful eyes. He arrived wearing a grimy jacket, standing at her doorway like a salesman, the kind she always turned away. As she shook his hand Ashley felt there was no grip to it, as if he affected a lack of threat in his manners. She briefly wondered if that helped with the job, making him inconspicuous as he spied on others' lives. His black hair was cut short and seemed pasted to his scalp like plastic that had melted. As he sat down on Ashley's sofa she wondered if it was a made up name. When she looked at him she felt slightly dirty, as if she'd invited a stranger into her home to share sexual secrets. She reminded herself that his services would settle her anxieties once and for all.

'Miss Rogers, you mentioned that you want your boyfriend followed,' he said.

'I want to find out if he's seeing other women.'

'It's a request I get asked all the time. I'll need his address and a picture.'

'Well that's the thing, I don't have it, his address.'

'Do you have a picture?'

'I have a few of them.'

She went and got the shots she'd printed up for him.

'Can you get his address?' Maurice said.

'I can call him I guess.'

She went into the kitchen and dialled his number and was surprised when he picked up.

'Julius I forgot to ask you for your address. I want to send you something.'

And so he gave it to her and she gave it to Maurice who put the piece of paper she wrote it on in his grimy pocket and went away after quoting her his fees. She gave him a down payment and then placed the order for a bottle of wine, one she knew Julius liked, to be sent to his flat in Kew that day with a message that read, 'Save this for the next time.'

Then she got ready to leave for a model shoot in London. She was still turning over in her mind what it was she couldn't fathom about Julius when she got there. She looked at some of the guys, great looking in their own way, but they lacked something Julius had and she tried to define what it was.

All day she thought about what Maurice Calm was doing and whether he would find anything out, and if so what. And she wondered if she'd still feel insecure if she had Julius all to herself. She craved him all through the session as she put on clothes and removed them, standing with other naked women among designer brands. They hung from their bodies like jewellery. The photographers snapped pictures, immersing them in strobe lighting fired from their lenses, phallic visual penetrations of their bodies as they strutted their stuff, all legs and arse, women on show, and inaccessible to touch. This was a sex show of sorts, the skin dance, the subtle suggestion of pussy, exotic erotic display of bodies forever young and forever desired.

That was it, she thought, as she got dressed to leave. She was used to being in the position Julius occupied in her mind. He gave so much in bed but it was what he held back that made her crave him even more. All the models in the room reserved something in their performance, and it was the immediacy of touch. As she watched them dress she wondered if these were the other women she feared Julius saw and whether he was into models.

28

Ashley rode home in a taxi, thinking of all the guys she'd known who were model chasers. Julius didn't fit the type. They were usually after a piece of fame. And the women knew it. Ashley didn't feel that with Julius. At her flat she poured a glass of Pinot Grigio and rang him as she slipped out of her skirt and stood in the kitchen in her panties, the phone in one hand, a glass in the other.

She got his voicemail and left a message asking him to call her, then she ran her hand along her skin imagining him there, with her all the time, removed from his other life. But it was Julius she wanted inside her at that moment and not her finger and the orgasm she induced in herself and which left her feeling a numb rage that she tried to rinse away by showering and dressing. She put on a long blue dress and some earrings. When Julius rang she asked him to take her out to eat. And so she went to Kew, to his flat, the place being watched by Maurice Calm, and she tried to detect signs of other women who'd been there as he got ready, but she found none.

Instead she found a new level to her desire as over dinner at a local Italian restaurant she saw a woman, beautiful, young, eye Julius with undisguised interest. He didn't return the look, pleasing Ashley. They walked to his flat beneath the still blue summer sky, and as soon as they were inside she began tearing off her clothes. Then they were naked in his bed and she lay back as he entered her. There was hunger and fear in her touch as she tried to push away the thought of other women, and she came deeply, without rage. They made love all night and when it was time for her to leave and drive home in the deserted streets she had one last look in the bathroom for lipstick or any signs that he was lying to her, but she found none.

It brought her little reassurance because Ashley's obsession that Julius was seeing other women was too deeply lodged inside her now, almost as if she wanted to discover it was true. And as she lay in the dark she asked herself what she would do if it were. How would she react if Maurice Calm returned with pictures of his affairs? And she knew she wouldn't end it, she wanted him too much. So why was she looking? Because she wanted to remove them.

The next morning she recalled what she thought during the night. She stared at herself in the mirror, and looked beneath her beautiful face for the potential.

And she asked herself could she kill and would she for this man about whom she knew so little and whose ability to give her pleasure was so dangerous. Murder would lead to his loss if she was caught, and she pondered the possibility of killing without detection. She wondered if she was going a little mad, high on him. Or was it love she felt, alone at home, beautiful Ashley whom all men desired and who was now caught on a hook.

29

Tuesday 2:00 PM.

Ever since Micky had said he'd deal with whoever put the tracking device in his Bentley, Karen had wondered what he would do. The cupboard full of knives had left her feeling more afraid of him than before, as if by unlocking it he was ushering her into his other life, the one in which she thought he killed. Who was Micky preying on? He'd held the door open for her and grinned at her. And in the few moments he afforded her to see his collection of weapons, she thought she saw a dark stain on one blade, a long serrated knife with a worn handle. She had no doubt he could kill. Micky made calls, went out for short trips that left Karen feeling frustrated his absences weren't longer. That afternoon she went into the kitchen where he was sitting at the table she tried to ascertain when he would be going away again. Her questions stirred his suspicions.

'What is this, why do you want to know?' he said.

'Because I don't like it when you go away.'

'Oh yeah? And why is that, you miss me do you?'

'I don't feel safe here alone.'

'You've got the dogs.'

'They don't obey me.'

'They'll chew your heart out.'

'Keep them on their chain Micky.'

'That won't work, I'll unshackle them when I go away, anyone breaking in here will become their supper, imagine them sinking their teeth into the bone.'

'I don't have your kind of thoughts.'

'What thoughts do you have?'

'I don't want those dogs walking round, they frighten me.'

'Do I frighten you Karen?'

'A little.'

'And why is that?'

'Because of the things you do.'

'With my hands you mean?'

'I don't like it when you, you know.'

'Touch you?'

'Put your fingers down your throat.'

'Would you prefer me to put them somewhere else?'

He got up from the chair and put his hand in her hair and stared into her face. His eyes looked like tiny pieces of glass.

'I don't think about violence, Micky.'

'I know what you think about,' he said, taking his hand away and wagging his finger at her.

She watched as he got a slice of bread and put it in the toaster, turning and leaning on the counter with his arms crossed and that scar of a grin he wore when he was thinking of things that made her blood run cold, things Karen felt forced to watch him do, because she knew what he would do if she walked away. She knew the look, the prelude to an act of insanity and menace. The smell of toast filled the room as she tried to think of ways to reach him. Micky took the toast, placed it gently on a plate, then got butter and raspberry jam from the fridge. He removed two knives from a drawer and sat down. Then he buttered the toast with one knife and and smeared jam across its surface with the other one, coating it until it dripped from the sides. Micky raised his eyes to hers as he took a bite, his chin turning red with the jam. He chewed then dipped his fingers in the jar and rose and walked towards her. Karen began to back away, but he grabbed her arm and smeared jam across her face. Then he kissed her, forcing his tongue into her mouth.

'That's sex for you,' he said.

He rubbed the rest of the jam in the jar across his face and put his head between her legs like a dog, as if he was smelling her sex, butting her and pushing her into the wall.

'I'll buy you honey,' Karen said, 'to stop you running from the bees.'

Micky raised his head.

'I'll shoot your babies if you do, and coat them in jam,' he said.

'I don't have any babies, I'm sterile.'

She yelled it and he took a step back.

'You're lying.'

'You know that we can't have children.'

'This is our placenta, Karen, the seeds I coat you with.'

'No, Micky this is all about bees and what you did all those years ago.'

'What's the real reason you don't feel safe?'

'This is a big house and you leave me alone, you don't tell me when you're coming back.'

'I'll get you a gun.'

'What?'

'Yeah, that'll sort you out, something easy to use.'

'Micky.'

But he walked away. Later that day he handed her the light Ruger pistol. He took her to the sound proofed building at the end of the garden. He showed her how to load it, and how to shoot. He set up some targets and she did well. Micky patted her arse afterwards and gave her that look.

'I always found a woman with a gun in her hand a turn on, let's have a shag,' he said.

'Here?'

'Why, do you want someone else, another man?

'No.'

'There better not be,' he said.

He snarled the last words, and his teeth reminded her of the dogs'.

'There isn't.'

'Then show me how much you want it.'

She did, trying to distract him from his violence, letting him pull up her skirt, and pull her panties to one side as he slid it in, the room full of oil and smoke. She stared over his back at the bullet holes in the wall. She thought of Julius, of his lovemaking and she felt pain, Micky's thrusts were brutal and humiliating, she was his to use and she hated herself for it. He put his hand inside her bra and as he touched her she felt as though he was smearing hatred on her skin. His touch was aggressive, proprietorial. His gaze was invasive. Suddenly he was stepping back and fumbling with his zip. Then they were outside and Karen watched him bend and stroke his dogs with a gentleness that almost broke her heart.

'Why don't you touch me like that?' Karen said.

'What, like an animal?'

'You treat me like one.'

'If you're not careful I'll chain you up out here.'

They went back inside the house. Micky opened a drawer in the kitchen and removed a skewer.

'Time for your tattoo,' he said.

'I'm not having a tattoo.'

'Skirt up. I'll use this on your buttocks.'

'Do you really think I'm going to let you cut me with that?'

'It won't hurt and besides, you let me do other things.'

'Put it away Micky.'

'Do you want me to strip it off you?'

'I'm not doing it.'

He came over to her and pulled at her skirt but Karen backed away. He held the skewer in front of her face, twisting it back and forth between his fingers.

'It keeps meat together, that's what it does. I'll trace the letters carefully across your flesh.'

'Like you're branding me.'

'It'll keep you in place while I'm away.'

'I'm not meat Micky.'

'Any man seeing that on your arse will know.'

'No man sees my arse apart from you.'

'He'll know I own you.'

'You can't do a tattoo with that, you need a needle.'

Micky nodded and walked away. Karen heard him go into his office and make more calls and she thought about the tracking device that had failed to deliver what she wanted to know, the piece of information she believed would free her of Micky and let her have Julius to herself. Since he'd found the device she hadn't dared hire a detective to have him followed. But now she recalled what she said to Julius and realised it was the only way. She'd kept the name and number in her handbag. When Micky went out late that afternoon she called Tammy.

30

Wednesday 11:00 AM.

They met at Tammy's office. Micky had told Karen he would be out all day at a meeting, he didn't say what nor did she ask. Karen gave her pictures of Micky and his Bentley's number plate. She gave her their address and told her what she knew of his movements.

'What is it you suspect you husband of doing?' Tammy said.

'This is a little strange,' Karen said.

'Do you think he's having an affair? That's not what I do.'

'No I read about you, I think he's a serial killer.'

Tammy leaned forward in her chair.

'What makes you say that?'

'There's violence in Micky, I think he hates women, and he's leading a double life. He goes away on trips, he's angry before he goes, calm when he returns.'

'And you don't think he's seeing another woman?'

'I don't.'

'Why not?'

'I found blood on his shirt, he takes a knife with him when he goes.'

'How long are the trips?'

'A few days usually.'

'You have no idea where he goes?'

'It's out of London, I know what much.'

'He told you this?'

'I placed a tracking device in his Bentley.'

'Whereabouts out of London?'

'I don't know, it tracked him out of the city then blanked out, he found it.'

'Does he suspect you of putting it there?'

'No, he thinks it's a business rival.'

'What does your husband do?'

'Micky made his money out of the building trade, but now I don't know what he does, he's evasive. I think he's selling weapons.'

'The knife you say he takes with him, what does it look like?'

'It's a long handled boning knife.'

Tammy stood up and walked over to the window and stared out at the street below. Then she turned to look at Karen in her neat blue suit, her hands folded on her lap. Tammy believed Karen thought her husband was a killer, but that didn't make him one. She didn't want to take on another case unless she was sure, she wanted time to track The Pimp.

'Is there anything else he does that makes you think he's a killer?' Tammy said.

'He has a cupboard in the house.'

'A cupboard?'

'He always kept it locked then the other day he showed me what he keeps in it. It's packed with knives.'

Tammy nodded, pursing her lips.

'I'll take the job,' she said.

She told Karen her charges and Karen handed her a wad of cash, money she'd taken from her account and that she'd claim she spent on clothes if Micky asked. She had enough of them hidden at the back of a wardrobe, items which she'd never worn. She'd wear them now. She'd let him fuck her like a hooker while she had him followed.

31

Arlene was out when Karen visited the office. When she returned Karen had gone and it was raining. There were drops of water on her hair and face which Tammy thought made her look even more beautiful. She wanted to brush them away from her skin with the back of her hand.

She told Arlene about the job she had just taken on. Tammy felt high on the sense that it may lead her to The Pimp. Karen's husband had a lot of the profile that matched him, especially the obsession with knives and his view of women. She'd often wondered if The Pimp was married.

They left the office at 5:00 PM and returned home, where they had a light dinner. Tammy had got a private lab to test the blood on the piece of what The Pimp claimed were Holly's panties. The results showed that it was Holly's blood. She'd checked the IP address on the camera she found in the bathroom, but it led nowhere. The Pimp had used a proxy server. As Arlene ran a bath Tammy felt that with the new job she'd taken on that day she was about to get the upper hand on the man who always evaded her and knew everything she did. And it felt great. Her sense of triumph didn't last long. When she went into the bathroom and looked down at Arlene in the water she reached her hand in and touched her, feeling her desire swell. Then she remembered what The Pimp had said to her about Holly. And she realised she was doing what he wanted her to do.

She wondered if he was watching her do this to her sister's lover, watching her touch her, watching Arlene reach her hand up and touch Tammy's breasts, watching as Tammy stripped out of her blouse and jeans and got in the water, unable to stop herself, needing the physical sensations she'd longed for and repressed for too long. The cameras had been removed, she told herself.

That is what Tammy thought as she kissed Arlene on the mouth. They went into the bedroom and made love on the tangled sheets. Arlene arched her back and dug her hand into Tammy's hair. And without knowing it Tammy stared at the camera hidden in the wall as The Pimp poured himself a cognac and drank to his success, studying their bodies, Arlene's white, pure, almost virginal but with the style and movement of a whore. He zoomed in on Tammy and her muscled physique, her large breasts. He was making a film of them. This was the cinema of secret pleasures, The Pimp's own film, where his actors did what he told them to.

He had many films there in the observation tower, a bare room full of flickering computer screens and data. He collected data on the women he planned to kill, but first of all he studied them, slowly engaging in their lives, and watching their desires. He liked to see them having sex, where they showed their natures. That was when he planned how he would kill them.

He was tall, as Joyce had described him, and his eyes were almost translucent, as if he were beyond observation. His face was not unhandsome. He was strong and moved with a calculated certainty. His hands were large, he had greying hair swept back on his forehead, and his complexion was pale.

He watched as Tammy walked naked into the kitchen and poured herself and Arlene a glass of Pinot Grigio. He listened to them talk, the two lesbians he had handpicked for his next murder. It would be his first double killing. He zoomed in on Tammy's parted legs as she sat on the sofa.

They talked, they went to bed. The Pimp made his film, he made it deep into the watchful night.

32

Ashley called Julius as rain swept into London and water pooled on the pavements, spilling off the kerbs as pedestrians hopped across puddles.

'I need to see you,' she said, trying to keep her voice steady.

'Today is a little hard.'

'Try for me Julius. Just for an hour.'

'I'll come round to your flat.'

He did. Turned up in a raincoat, took it off, stood there in her hall in a blue shirt and jeans, so casual, so desirable even underdressed as he was then. She asked him how his plans to move in with her were going. He told her he was nearly there, it shouldn't be long. The answers slid off his tongue like honey, and she felt he was being evasive.

'So you'll move in next week?' she said.

'Yes, I think that works.'

She tried to read his indigo eyes. But she couldn't, and instead she touched his chest, running her fingers across his skin, and they went upstairs.

He made deep long love to her on her bed and she came twice, then she mounted him, clenching her ankles around his legs. She didn't let go until he came. This was the tacit reassurance she sought from their physical encounters, one signal physical proof of his desire. And she asked herself why she doubted it. The sex was steamy enough. But she needed to take that from him, as if it was assurance that he wouldn't spend it elsewhere.

After he left she drank a bottle of wine and called her friends to go out to a club. Two guys tried to pick her up but she declined, thinking only of Julius, with the impenetrable mind and the ability to fuck her like no other man. She thought about Maurice Calm, watching him, gathering information on his other life. She would call him first thing in the morning.

And so she did, getting Maurice as he was entering his office.

'I was wondering what you've found out,' she said.

'Not much. His habits are pretty regular.'

'What does that mean? You haven't seen him with other women?'

'Not yet.'

'What are his habits?'

'He doesn't go out much, he met a man and they seemed to be talking business.'

'No women?'

'Not yet.'

Ashley felt high after the call, but waited to see if Maurice would unearth the other women she was so convinced were there in Julius's life. But if he was telling the truth then she had what she wanted, she had Julius and it was only a matter of time before she could penetrate him. If he lived with her then whatever it was he was hiding would yield to her view. She wanted to place him under surveillance. She wanted to watch his every move. Because she insistently knew there was something there, something different that she needed to identify. His sexual appeal remained a danger until she did.

33

Friday 9:30 AM.

Micky went away that Friday, walked into the kitchen as Karen was having breakfast and made the announcement. He always did it at the last minute, she thought. He liked surprising her, which he did in many ways, from his erratic movements to his sexual demands.

'It won't be long,' he said.

'Back on Monday are you?'

'You think I'd tell you that? Why do you want to know?'

'I thought you wanted me to know.'

'Did you?'

'Micky.'

'You got a gun now Karen, you got dogs with sharp teeth to protect you.'

'Do you think I want to shoot someone?'

'Who comes to this house?'

'No one.'

'That's not true, we have business colleagues over.'

'Yes and you set the dogs on them.'

'I was protecting you.'

'No you weren't, you were teaching him a lesson.'

'Do you want me to teach you a lesson?'

'I want you to tell me when you will be back.'

'You'll love the tattoo.'

'I am not having one.'

'Why? I'm the only one who'll see it.'

'No.'

'I'm going to give it to you myself, I'm learning all about needles and pain.'

'You could infect me.'

'You can use anything you know. I'll use a splinter of glass from a shattered jam jar.'

'Not on me you're not.'

'What have you got against tattoos?'

'Just because you want to put one on your chest it doesn't mean I want one.'

'I haven't got a tattoo.'

'The other night over the cut. You showed it to me in bed.'

'Look.'

He raised his shirt and she saw only scars.

'It wasn't a real tattoo.'

'Do you think I'd do that to my skin? I washed it off, like I wash you off my skin when I go away.'

'I think it's me who needs to do the washing.'

'You're up to something.'

'No.'

'So why the snooping?'

'Is it snooping for a wife to want to know when her husband will come back?'

'That's not what I'm talking about.'

'What then?'

'You know what I mean.'

'I don't.'

'You're a sexual spy Karen.'

'What does that mean?'

But he didn't answer, he left, and she heard his Bentley crunch the gravel on the drive and the gates swing shut. Then she called Julius, who was stepping out of the shower.

She drove round that afternoon and Maurice Calm snapped her on his Nikon as she rang Julius's bell. He snapped the kiss he gave her at the doorway, but not what happened upstairs, although he timed how long she was up there before they went out to eat. Julius made love to her for two hours before they did.

They ate a local French restaurant then returned to his flat. Julius noticed the car parked outside and the man sitting behind the wheel, his gaze averted as they passed by. They went up into his living room where Karen talked about Micky. She told Julius about the conversation she'd had with him. He listened and at one point got up and walked over to the window. He looked down at the man sitting in the driver's seat.

'He found the tracking device,' Karen said.

'Do you think he knows you planted it?' he said.

'I'm not sure any more. Maybe he knows about us.'

'He's playing a game with you.'

'I don't even know if he has gone away.'

'Aren't you taking a risk?

'I had to see you.'

'What would he do if he found out?'

'I think he'd kill you.'

'You're convinced he's a killer.'

'I hired someone, she's following him now, I asked her to call me if he returns home.'

'We're being watched, there's a man in a car outside with a camera. Do you think your husband has hired someone to follow you?'

'He can't know about us. I've been too careful.'

'Maybe not careful enough.'

She started to walk over to the window when Julius put his hand on her shoulder.

'Don't let him know we've seen him.'

'What does he look like?'

'Hard to say from this distance.'

'When did you notice him?'

'When we went out to eat.'

'You said he has a camera.'

'I caught a glimpse of it in his hand.'

'What car is it?'

'Some kind of Ford.'

'Well if it's not Micky who's behind this, then it has to be do with you.'

'I can't think of why someone would want to spy on me.'

'A husband of another woman.'

34

'There are no other women, Karen.'

She held his gaze then looked away. She didn't believe him, but she didn't care any more. She wanted him and she wanted to get rid of Micky. With him gone she could make sure she was the only one. Julius poured them another glass of wine each then they went into the darkened bedroom. From the window there they got another angle on the car and the man inside it. He was talking on his mobile phone. The burning tip of a cigarette was clenched between his fingers.

'I'm going to go down and talk to him,' Julius said.

'Is that a good idea?'

'It'll put an end to it one way or another. Do you have any cash on you?'

'A few hundred in my purse.'

She gave it to him and watched as he went out into the street.

Maurice Calm was talking to his boyfriend. They shared a basement flat in Fulham. His boyfriend was a good few years younger than him and Maurice kept him. He sometimes spied on him, jealous of the time he spent alone and the ease with which he could see other men. Maurice liked a certain kind of man. Until that afternoon he hadn't seen Julius do anything worth reporting back to Ashley. Now he felt he'd got the information she wanted. He'd call her later. The shots he'd taken were clear enough. He glanced up at the window of Julius's flat as he hung up. Then he heard the passenger door open and Julius got in.

'Going somewhere?' Julius said.

'What do you think you're doing?'

Julius reached across the seat and took hold of the camera that was wedged against Maurice's thigh. As he did Maurice looked at him and became aroused. This guy was gorgeous, the best looking man he'd ever seen. He watched as Julius looked at the pictures he'd taken of him kissing the woman in the doorway.

'They're clear enough for your client. I can pay you more than he is,' Julius said.

'It'll cost you two thousand.'

'Here's two hundred, I can get you the rest tomorrow. I delete the pictures.'

'Not until you pay me.'

'Too late.'

Julius held him at arm's length, pushing Maurice into the seat as he wiped the evidence from the camera.

'If you don't want me to tell my client, there's something else you'll have to do,' Maurice said.

'What's that?'

Maurice looked at him, so casual, so good-looking, but straight, and he wanted to corrupt him. As Maurice unzipped his fly he wondered if the turn on was caused by the man's looks or the idea of what he was about to ask him to perform. Either way he wanted to take full advantage of the situation. It wasn't the first time he'd been rumbled, but never like this.

'I'm not doing it,' Julius said.

'Then I'll report back what I saw.'

'Without the evidence, I don't think he'll like that.'

'What makes you think it's a he?'

'Who is she then?'

'Do what I'm asking and I'll tell you.'

'No.'

'I'll come back in another car. I'm good at this.'

'Not good enough, you won't get any more on me.'

Julius got out and walked away. He heard the engine of the Ford start up and the car drift off into the darkness of the surrounding streets.

'I got rid of the pictures he took,' he said to Karen when he got upstairs.

'What were the pictures?'

'A couple of you ringing on my bell. Me kissing you at the door.'

'It's got to be Micky.'

'It's not.'

'Who then?'

'I owe some money.'

'Who to? So this is about you, is it a woman?'

'No. I invested in a business scheme and lost a lot of cash.'

'Why would someone send a detective after you?'

'I put in an insurance claim. They're checking up on me.'

'So it's not Micky?'

'No, he told me who sent him.'

'Why did he do that?'

'I threatened to call the police. The insurance company sent him.'

'But why take pictures of me?'

'These guys are told to get as much information as possible.'

'How much money did you lose?'

'Thousands.'

'Are you in trouble?'

'Only financially.'

'Then Micky doesn't know.'

Julius knew who had sent him before he left the car. He wondered what the detective would tell Ashley but he already had his story straight.

35

10:00 PM.

Karen went back that night, still concerned the detective had been sent by Micky. The house was empty and she called Julius, but he was engaged. He was talking to Ashley. She'd rung him first thing after she'd put down the phone to Maurice Calm. He had told her he saw Julius with a woman, but that his cover had been blown.

'It was my sister,' Julius said.

'He said you kissed her.'

'Yes on the cheek. That should be clear in the shots he took.'

'There aren't any, he said you destroyed them.'

'He's lying.'

'Tell me again what happened.'

'I was over by the window when I saw him, he was obvious.'

'How did you know he was a detective?'

'I didn't at first. There have been some burglaries so I decided to go down and get his number plate.'

'He said you got in the car.'

'He was pointing the camera at my window, I asked him what he was doing.'

'What did he say?'

'He didn't say anything, he tried to drive off.'

'With you in the car. Are you telling me the truth?

'I threatened to call the police, I got out and that was that.'

'So the woman is really your sister?'

'Yes. I've been wondering what it was all about.'

'Why would he lie to me?'

'When did you hire him?'

'Over a week ago.'

'He's lying to you because he hasn't got anything on me, and he wants more money.'

'You've never mentioned a sister.'

'Ashley, we haven't known each other that long.'

'I'm sorry. I shouldn't have done it.'

'Why did you?'

'I thought you were seeing other women.'

'And if you found out I was what then?'

'I don't know, are you?'

'No.'

'You'll still move in?'

'I don't know, Ashley.'

36

11:00 PM.

Karen tried again an hour later and got through, feeling angry she'd gone home and no sign of Micky.

'Come over,' Julius said, casual, nothing to hide, Karen liked that, wondering who he'd been talking to for so long.

She got dressed, feeling high, drove there beneath a deep blue sky that promised heat the next day, and they went out to eat. They went to a bistro, and they drank red wine late into the night, Karen feeling young again, wanting more, and pushing away the constriction on her life that was her marriage. She thought about the detective and if he had been sent by Micky.

'No strangers hanging around outside?' Karen said.

'He won't be back.'

'I was sure it was Micky. I was so worried.'

'And now?'

'I'm not.'

Karen ordered a steak, rare, with fries, Julius chicken breast with vegetables. She kicked her shoes off under the table and ran her foot up his leg. When they left, the streets were deserted and they went to bed. The next morning they woke early and Julius made love to her before they had breakfast.

Julius was pouring her a second glass of coffee when her phone rang. She glanced at the caller ID and saw Tammy's name.

'Hello, Tammy?' Karen said, glancing at Julius, alarm in her eyes.

'I know it's taken a while to get back to you but he's been evasive.'

'It's OK. Do you have something on him, where is he?'

'He's at an address outside London.'

'He's not on his way home?'

'I don't think he'll be leaving today. Your husband is not a killer.'

'Why do you say that?'

'Because of what I just saw.'

'What?'

'Did you know he's gay?'

'Micky gay?'

'He's visiting his boyfriend. I just saw them kissing, that's what he's been hiding from you, but there's something else, you were right about violence being part of it.'

37

The whole of Sunday Karen tried to digest the idea that Micky was leading a secret life as a gay with a partner. It made sense, it explained his behaviour in bed, the conflict he felt. Tammy had suggested she come in Monday morning to hear the rest, reluctant to go into it on the phone, mentioning bugging. That made Karen anxious.

Tammy had mentioned there was something else on the phone and Karen heard it that morning at Tammy's office as sunlight blasted the windows and gave the room a strange high definition quality that accentuated the sharp reality of what she discovered about her husband. Tammy closed the door and placed some pictures on the desk. She watched as Karen stared at Micky with another guy, younger than him by ten years or more. Micky kissing him in some of them. It was like it wasn't him, it didn't look like Micky, there was pleasure in his face, the thing he hid from her.

'Do you know who he is?' Tammy said.

'The boyfriend?'

Karen stared at the face, handsome, rough, eyes as cold as hailstones, a thin smile showing sharp white teeth.

'He's a dangerous man,' Tammy said.

'I've never seen him before.'

'He's a gangster who's behind various hits that have been carried out across London. You didn't see the articles in the papers.'

'No, who is he?'

'Gary Krane.'

Tammy slid a copy of The Times across the desk and watched as Karen picked it up and read about the hits. Businessmen had been taken out across London in a series of assassinations that targeted either men with interests in some of Krane's businesses or men who had threatened to expose him as a criminal.

'Micky was involved with some of these guys, I recognise the names,' Karen said.

'You mean the targets?'

'That's right, we even entertained one of them for dinner.'

'You were right that he's leading a double life, but he's not a killer. You were close though, he's involved with one.'

'He must have started seeing him a few years ago, now I think about it. How did he get involved with him?'

'My guess is Micky went to him to carry out a hit.'

'Why does he take a knife with him?'

'They're involved in violent sex with other gays. I got some pictures on Sunday, shots of a party they held. It's disturbing. They get young men round and hand out booze and pills, these are guys with addictive problems they use for sex. Then Gary Krane starts to get rough. This is where Micky's violence comes in. He likes cutting them.'

'You mean he slashes the guests?'

'Yeah, they're numb from drugs, Krane pays them to keep quiet. I think Micky's obsession with knives has found an outlet with a man who is a sadist.'

'You said that Micky is involved with a killer, but from what I've read Gary Krane pays other people to do it for him.'

'He does. But he also committed at least two murders, gangland stuff.'

'It says the police arrested him.'

'They did, for the two murders, then let him go because they didn't have any proof.'

'So if I took this to the police it wouldn't help?'

'No.'

'I was hoping I could use this to leave him,' Karen said.

'You've met someone else?'

'Yes, but I need something the police can use on Micky. And this isn't it.'

'You're not in danger so long as he doesn't suspect you know.'

'Do you think you can find out something about him that I can take to the police?'

'I can try, Karen.'

'He doesn't know he's been followed?'

'No one knows when I follow them.'

'What can you find out?'

'I can see if I can tie him to any of the hits. Gary is involved in a lot of criminal activity and Micky may be implicated.'

'I think Micky is involved in arms deals.'

'That wouldn't surprise me.'

'I've seen some papers lying on his desk, overheard things when he's on the phone.'

'Gary Krane is involved in a lot worse than arms dealing.'

'How does he get away with it?'

'He gives orders through a long line, so he's removed from any crime.'

'But the police know it's him?'

'They know but they can't do anything about it.'

'He said he'd be back today. I'll let you know as soon as he tells me he's going away again.'

'I need to keep him under surveillance.'

'Permanently?'

'Most of the time.'

'Do you think he's committing crimes in London?'

'I think it's more than likely.'

'But what?'

'Gary Krane is not going to be easy to put away, and if you use this against Micky then Gary will come after you. My opinion is your husband has problems but he is involved with a man who is far more dangerous than him. Watching them, I got the feeling that Micky is trying to please Gary. He hates himself for it and takes it out on you.'

'That makes sense, the way he is when he gets back from visiting him.'

'There is one way to get Gary Krane put away, and that is to identify a hit man he uses, he'd bring Krane down with him,' Tammy said.

'The papers said a series of hits had been carried out, he must use more than one.'

'Yes, but there's one he favours for the difficult jobs, a man known as Hundred Percent, the reason being he has never failed in a hit, never left any evidence behind him, and the police have no idea who he is. There is no CCTV footage of him entering or leaving premises where assassinations have been carried out, but the police do have a recording of Gary Krane on the phone where he says, "Hundred Percent will take him out." The man he was referring to was shot in the head the next day at his office.'

'When will you start your surveillance again?' Karen said.

'This week, I'll be watching him at your house too. I want to put a bug on your land line, is that OK?'

'It's fine with me.'

'How about I come round this afternoon while Micky is away?'

Karen went home and ate some lunch, thinking of what Micky was into, her mouth dry, the sour taste of bile seeping into her palate. If he was screwing other men, what was he risking, could he be carrying something? As she chewed on a piece of tinned tuna she felt something sharp pierce her tongue. She pulled a tiny fish bone from the mayonnaise that adhered to the bread in her mouth, a drop of blood bulging from its tip, and she thought how slender her future with Julius was.

She felt angry and betrayed and glad and sick at the same time, wanting to push away her feelings as a wife and replace them with a pragmatism that would enable her to rid herself of Micky. He hated women, she was right about that. But he needed her, he needed the pretence of a marriage and so he punished her for his sexual disgust with the female body. That was why he rarely looked at her when he entered her. That was why he kept her chained, because he would never accept another man in her life, it would constitute a failure on his part to control her. She wondered if he saw his lover's face as he penetrated her. And she realised she didn't care. Perhaps Gary would kill him for her. And as she thought that she knew that was what she wanted and she pushed it away. Tammy would find something out, something that Karen could take to the police. She would have Julius to herself. She told herself all these things as she poured herself a glass of wine and heard the doorbell ring. Then Karen took Tammy into Micky's office and watched as she bugged his private line.

38

Micky turned up that evening. He walked into the kitchen where Karen was reading a newspaper, kissed her on the cheek then went upstairs and took a shower. When he came down he sat at the table watching her, Karen glancing at him, Micky studying her face. Then he said it.

'I know you're seeing a fella.'

'I'm not.'

'You are. I know it Karen, I can tell.'

'I am not seeing anyone.'

'Good looking is he?'

'There isn't anyone Micky.'

'Upstairs then.'

'No.'

'You must be gagging for it.'

'I'm tired of this.'

He grabbed her by the wrist and dragged her to the bedroom.

'I got something to show you,' he said.

He went into the spare room and she heard him unlock the cupboard. He returned holding a knife, the one she thought she saw a stain on, but it was spotless now, and the overhead light caught the steel which flashed brightly in Micky's hand. He began to move like a Matador, his movements exaggerated, holding the knife above his head in a bizarre ritual of masculine show. Karen thought of him and Gary Krane. Then Micky began to undo his shirt. He stood only a few feet from her, and placed the tip of the blade on his right nipple, pressing until a bead of blood dripped dark red from the pink skin. There was a look of savagery on his face coupled with the pleasure of the guilty man finding release in pain.

'What would you say to a man with no nipples?' Micky said.

'Why would you do that to yourself, mutilate your body Micky?'

'I think they're for women. I think nipples make me like a woman.'

'And you'd never want to be one would you?'

He raised the dripping tip to within an inch of her right eye and Karen stood there knowing he wouldn't cut her, knowing it was all show.

'No,' he said, 'would you want to be a man, for an hour and make me kneel?'

'Why would I want to make you kneel?'

'Because you want to do things to me, penetrate my skin.'

'Micky I don't have your need to do that sort of thing.'

'Think I'm mental do you?' he said, pointing the knife at his temple now.

'No, I think you're troubled.'

'By what?'

'What happened.'

'You're on about bees again.'

'There's no honey in the house.'

'I know a man who reminds me of that boy.'

'Who, Micky?'

'A man with a dark obsession. He does things, things even I find hard to watch.'

'What does he do?'

'He rearranges people's skins.'

'You're talking about cutting again.'

'I'm talking about love.'

A fly buzzed past his head and Micky swung at it. Then he laid the knife on the bed and put his fingers in his mouth. His face looked like a mask as he forced his hand inside. Karen thought of his other life, of his affair with a violent man. And Micky gazed at her as he touched the back of his throat and began to choke. He pulled his hand out.

'I want to pull them out but they're lodged too deeply in,' he said.

'Who's been scaring you Micky?'

He went over to the bed and began to caress the edge of the knife with the tip of his forefinger, looking at Karen as he did.

'Remember how you used to touch me? That's what this is.'

'No it's not, Micky, it's a knife, it's not skin.'

Karen looked at him standing there, and she understood what lay behind his need to humiliate her. He was trying to prove his heterosexuality to himself, through her, his wife. His ownership of a woman was an attempt to reject the thing he hated in himself, namely his desire for men. His sex with her was a way of separating himself from his other life.

Micky went into the bathroom and stuck a plaster on his cut, put his shirt on and left the bedroom. Karen could hear him on the phone in his office as she left the house.

39

She drove for a few miles then stopped in a deserted street and called Julius. She told him what Tammy had found out. She told him about Gary Krane and what Micky had done in the bedroom when he got home. She said she wasn't going to stop seeing him, but that she was worried Micky was going to have her followed.

'Do you think he knows or is he testing you?' Julius said.

'I'm not sure, but I don't want to take any chances right now.'

'Don't see me for a while. See what your detective finds out.'

'I'm not going to give you up.'

'You'll have to wait for him to go on another trip.'

'I'm worried, if he knows he'll have you killed.'

'I'm not worried about that.'

'Why not?'

'I think it's unlikely.'

'How can you be so confident?'

'Why do you think he's suddenly accused you of having an affair?'

'I don't know, I thought he might have known he was being followed'

'Call me when he goes away again.'

'I'll call you before then.'

'When you do come and see me you'll have to make sure there's no one on your tail.'

'How do I do that?'

'Take a different route, park streets away.'

40

Tuesday 8:00 AM.

The Pimp sent another parcel to Tammy, a box wrapped in a yellow ribbon. It arrived first thing. She opened it and stared at a pair of Holly's red stilettoes, ones she used to dance in. She was standing in the kitchen when Arlene walked in behind her and peered over her shoulder. The Pimp heard it all in high definition sound.

'Those were the shoes he raped me with,' Arlene said.

'He knows you're here with me.'

'Then he's still watching us. We haven't stopped his surveillance of us.'

'The company I used to sweep the house is one of the best.'

'They must have missed a camera.'

'Or he's got back in,' Tammy said.

'How could he have?'

'He knows the code to the alarm.'

'But you changed it.'

'Unless he has a camera trained on the house from the outside.'

Tammy gestured to Arlene to go outside. They put on their shoes and walked to the end of the street.

'How do we stop him?' Arlene said.

'If he hasn't got a camera on us then he's following us. I can tail him.'

'And what if he's not?'

'I'll get the house swept again.'

'It didn't work last time.'

'Unless he works for the company,' Tammy said.

'Use a different one.'

'I need to figure out when he's been in the house.'

'Put a camera outside.'

'I need the whole house covered if we're going to get a shot of him, Arlene.'

41

11:00 AM.

Ashley called Julius that morning, standing by the window of her living room with a glass of wine in her hand and tears in her eyes. It was only a Pinot Grigio, she told herself, nothing heavy, and she'd stop as soon as he moved in. She'd seen many models do a lot stronger things early before a shoot.

She told him how she wouldn't let it happen again. Julius listened, hearing the anxiety in her voice, Ashley trying to stay calm. She asked him to come over for lunch. He surprised her when he said he would. They made love in the bedroom. And she felt high on him. Afterwards they went downstairs and she made steak sandwiches for them and they drank red wine. And Ashley thought of how it would be, him there with her. She thought how she wouldn't feel jealous if he was living with her.

'Move in,' she said.

'Why don't we wait a little?'

'Just try it Julius. Live with me for a few weeks.'

'Are you going to keep spying on me?'

'No. But I don't want you seeing any other women.'

'There aren't any other women.'

'Do we have time for one more?'

'I don't see why not.'

Ashley got on the kitchen table and wrapped her legs around his waist. And she was once again the model everyone desired.

She tried to hold onto it, the flame that sustained her, but when Julius left she felt fractured again. She got ready for him to move in, making space in cupboards and looking at clothes she wore and thinking about the boyfriends she'd been with at the time. There had been a lot of men, and women. But none like Julius and she thought about what it was, the difference between him and the others. It was more than the mental distance he seemed to occupy. It was as if there was another Julius who existed below the surface of the man who made love to her, someone she didn't know. Perhaps that was where he was vulnerable to the kind of emotions she wanted him to feel.

She went out shopping to pass the time, looked at herself in the mirrors of changing rooms, knowing she had it all, the looks, the body, the sexual poise to pull anyone. And she felt a flicker of anger then, at how she was failing to coax Julius into the erotic position she needed a man to occupy in her heart. It was as she was travelling back in a taxi that it came to her how she would secure him in the way she wanted to. Ashley would engage in extreme sexual acts. That is how she would find the other man, the inner Julius. For it was him she hungered for beneath the smart seducer, the man she felt was a gigolo.

That was why she felt this craving, he was hiding himself from her, giving her his body and only that, the way some women did with men. She thought of him, the other Julius, she thought of all the things he felt and would say to her beneath their sheets that smelt of sex. Ashley began to arrange in her mind the acts she would perform for him to find a way to his head. And as she did she felt a sense of arousal second only to the sensations Julius imbued her body with, long, languishing acute agonised pleasure that was like fire on the erotic nerves.

Ashley wanted to enter him, as if some part of her were consumed by the masculine sexual urge. To penetrate this man who remained beyond the reach of her female allure. To be inside him the way he was with her every time he fucked her. And she would see what he craved in bed, she would fill him with the craving she felt every day since he first entered her body with his mind. As Ashley thought all these things she became wet with passion.

The idea of having him this way remained with her during the entire day and through the evening. She was high on arousal, vanishing into Eros, a stranger to pain. All through the night she wanted to feel his body pressed against hers. He was the wandered sex god, the hidden man with hidden wants. And if she found him, if she had him what would that entail, Ashley wondered. For it was hard to imagine a greater high than he already gave to her in bed, but now she felt she was about to find Julius's sexual heart. She pictured its tapestry, a rich and dripping body of sexual colour, a synaesthesia of sensations. And she imagined the orgasms her body would enjoy, alone with only him and his craving.

As Ashley got up the following morning she wondered what he would crave if it wasn't her. And the answer seemed obvious, once she had tethered him he would only crave her and no one else. That was, after all, what she wanted. That was the reason he would move in with her so she could penetrate the inner man and find his mind. That was where her solace lay, beyond the distant Julius. That was where her real pleasure lay, inside him, and she would know his thoughts, the ones he hid, all of them. She could count them on a chain and wear them to bed and he would touch her in the dark.

There was an inner way he would fuck her, she knew that as she got dressed, seeing Julius naked and inside her. And she would reach him and keep him in her flat.

She called him that afternoon, and asked him when he was moving in, sounding calm, even to herself. And she was surprised by his answer, coming as readily as it did.

'Any time you want,' he said.

'Today.'

Two hours later he arrived with a case, stepped out of a taxi and rang her bell, Ashley watching it all from the living room window, high.

She sat on the bed and watched him put his clothes in the wardrobe, loving it, wanting him to do it to her right there. And he did, Julius ever aware of her needs.

She made them some dinner, a salad and some cold cuts of meat, and she gazed at him there in her flat. And she hungered for the inner man.

She wondered if he would sound like Julius and look like Julius and she laughed at how silly she was being. He was right there, he would always look this way. It was his mind she wanted, for it was where his sex lay, beneath the body. And his body had such appeal, but coupled with his mind she would have it all, all of her lover, the man who knew women.

She could watch him now, she could watch beneath the flesh for those hidden things, and be aroused at them. She could touch him all day and he could fuck her all night. She would not need to worry about other women because there would be none, only her. Ashley felt high, and she began to tingle.

42

The film The Pimp was making of Tammy and Arlene was his director's cut of their inner sexual lives, the ones he knew about before they did. For The Pimp studied the women he killed. He studied them for tone and tendency, and watched them mount the arc of their desires. He enjoyed stirring them to sensations they sought only in their sleep. And once they had performed the acts he knew they needed to commit he came for them. Because The Pimp knew what they wanted, they needed him to show them. They loved being on film, he would show them the images he'd taken when he used the knife on their bodies, nice white skins ready for the blade.

He penetrated them with cameras and watchfulness, dwelling at the threshold of their lives. He accumulated information and visual stimuli on them. Then he visited them and took them to places where he committed his indecent acts of sexual butchery. The final penetration was always with the knife.

He enjoyed the watching. His murderous urges came to the boil in the surveillance that was to him a killer's foreplay.

To alter them, to render them compliant to their repressed sexual urges was to make them his and on a level with the things he needed to do. Then to murder them.

He had Tammy naked, in the bath, masturbating, walking around her house half dressed. He had Tammy and Arlene engaged in lesbian acts. He watched the scenes again and again. He knew what Tammy wanted to do to her sister, and he edited and cut the film until they were the women he knew them to be.

Cutting the film was a thrill, it contained a form of sexual pleasure to The Pimp. But it was not as much a thrill as cutting their flesh.

He watched the film, and he made it into his film. Meanwhile Tammy and Arlene made love and The Pimp saw them doing the things he'd told them to do. These were the sexual acts he knew they wanted, the ones they secretly desired and dutifully repressed. He released them from that obligation and edged them towards his knife.

43

Tammy and Arlene were in the bedroom as he filmed them. Tammy was taking her clothes off, her movements slow, sexy. She shed blouse, bra, jeans and panties, laying them one by one on the chair as Arlene watched. She lay on the bed, then Arlene began to strip, taking off her skirt, then her blouse and bra and pulling down her G-string.

'Touch me the way you did it to Holly,' she said.

'Like this.'

But The Pimp felt strangely distracted from this peep show.

As Arlene showed Tammy the things she did to Holly and The Pimp watched, it evoked unwelcome memories. He did not like to dwell in the past, that place of bruises and humiliation. He watched them touch one another on his film of secret sexual desires. But as they did, another series of images was superimposing itself on their bodies.

At twenty-two he'd shot a woman in the leg while she was taking a shower. He'd watched her undressing and soaping up. His gun was wet from the spray of water as he fired, and it excited him. He'd stared at the bullet hole and inserted his finger in it, denying her vagina the same attention and then as she screamed he clamped his hand over her mouth and raped her. It was the best sexual experience he'd had until that point in his scarred life. He began to frequent prostitutes, often visiting two a day and asking them to engage in acts many refused. The Pimp found the desperate ones, so addicted to crack they allowed him to cut them, sometimes on the soles of their feet or legs.

Soon his urges grew more extreme and he turned to murder as a form of sexual release, since the things he wanted to do to women no prostitute would allow. His expertise with surveillance came from his skills as an alarm engineer. He first planted a hidden camera in the house of a woman whose alarm he'd fitted. He watched her bathe every day before raping and killing her with a kitchen knife taken from her drawer.

The shots he took of her did nothing to ally his thirst for more, and so he entered into the life of a watchful serial killer who existed beyond reach. He'd watched Holly dance for months before he abducted her, he liked her show, especially the one where she wore glasses and looked over their rims at the audience as she stuck a finger in herself, always at the front of the stage showing it all, unlike some of the others.

She was a good sexual victim who turned him on immensely and the sound of her skin as he cut it was melodic and staccato. And now he had her sister.

The Pimp watched Tammy and Arlene. But to him the real purpose of it all was to alter them. As he recalled shooting the woman in the shower what he saw was a small boy with wet trousers tied to chair in a bare room, his mouth sealed tight with duct tape while a woman with a scarred face scolded him. She stood above him wagging a finger at him.

The boy told himself scars were beautiful. But his tongue felt like wood in his mouth. Now he could almost feel the stinging sensation as she ripped the tape from his lips. Then suddenly her mouth moved and no sound came out of it. The Pimp looked at Tammy and Arlene. He heard the sound of tearing and imagined cutting their flesh and their erotic cries. This lesbian soldier would never find him. He had a drawer full of Holly to send to her a bit at a time, he had a room full of boxes and tissue paper. He wrapped up Holly and Tammy wrapped up her real desires. The Pimp knew them all, he was never fooled by the coyness of a whore, he would alter her by perpetual derangement and give Holy to her sister.

44

Micky strutted into the bedroom as Karen was getting dressed, recently showered, smelling of perfume. He watched as she placed a leg on the bed and put a stocking on, taking in the curve of her thigh. Karen paused, the other stocking in her hand and put her foot down on the floor. She was picking her bra up off the bed when Micky walked over to her.

'I like you in those,' he said.

'Then I'll finish getting dressed.'

'Leave the bra off. They still look good, your tits.'

'I've got to go out.'

'I thought we could have a drink.'

'It's the morning Micky.'

'Like that.'

'Like what?'

'Have a drink with you like that, half naked.'

'I'm cold.'

'How does that feel?' Micky said, touching her tits.

'I'm not in the mood.'

He shoved her on the bed and pulled down the single stocking, taking the other one from her hand. He unzipped his fly.

As he raped her she tried to scream but he stuffed the stocking in her mouth. When he got up he threw some pictures on the bed.

45

They were of Tammy. Shot after shot of Tammy in her car, of her with a camera zoomed in on a house, of her staking Micky out. He'd found out about her and Karen knew she was in danger. As she dressed and went downstairs she thought of what Tammy had said about not telling Micky what she knew.

'You see what I'm up against?' he said as she entered the kitchen.

'What is all this?'

'First the tracking device. Now he's put an investigator on me.'

'Who's doing this Micky?' Karen said.

'I don't know but I intend to find out.'

'What are you going to do?'

'Find out who she is, first of all, the woman who was taking the pictures.'

'Then what?'

'What do you think?'

'Well someone hired her.'

'I'll find out and hurt him.'

'So that's why you've been acting like that.'

'It's the only way I can get the stress out Karen, a quick shag, you understand.'

'Do you have to do it like that?'

There was laughter in Micky's eyes as he patted her arse and walked out of the room.

46

Ashley woke and looked at Julius lying there next to her, his face resting on the edge of her pillow. She studied him, his bronzed face, his body. The desire was not waning, she lived in a sexual addiction that was growing more intense. It would take her time to find his mind, she told herself as she lifted the sheets and looked at his cock. It was resting on his muscular thigh and she ran her finger along the shaft. Julius stirred and opened his eyes. She touched his face and kissed his lips, and she felt on fire again the way she had the first time. The fire had never gone away, and he stoked it every day with his looks and his touch.

He took her to the flame on which she mounted. He touched her breasts, and she leaned forward and he took her nipples in his mouth. So subtle, so erotic, she began to melt there in the early morning light, her naked body thrilled by what he did and what she knew he was going to do to her. And still he brought new things to the bedroom.

He kissed her mouth and Ashley reached down and felt his skin, his muscles, his arse, the heat rising from his body. She lay back and touched his cock and felt it stir as Julius slid his finger inside her. He entered her slowly, putting his cock inside her, deeper and deeper, all the way to Ashley's ecstasy. She drew him in, wrapping her toned thighs around his waist and she came. Then she mounted him, wanting to make him come, wanting to feel the hot liquid spurt inside her, pushing him down on the bed. She rode him hard, pushing until he came and then she put her tongue in his mouth.

These were the mornings of sexual addiction that made her body ache, these were the days of Ashley's exploring of the mind of the man who seduced her to the core. There was no way of knowing him simply through the sexual act, he defied that basic premise. It was one she'd used to mine her men for the desire she needed to see in their eyes. But with Julius it had no effect. She showered and watched him dress. And in every act he performed he was sexual in a way that amazed her now he was living with her. She'd expected an exposure of sorts, a lessening of his appeal, telling herself no one could be that good all the time. But he was and she realised it was not a performance. He inspired desire the way some women attract sexual advances. And she searched his eyes for the other Julius as she dried herself, showing him her naked dripping body, wanting him to want her. She looked for the hidden man and saw only the intense indigo of his gaze. She wanted more and more of him, his body and his touch. And she wondered where it would end, this desire that seemed to have no limit. She dressed and they went downstairs.

Over breakfast she looked at him and Ashley thought of the extreme sexual acts she would perform to find the inner Julius. And she thought of what she would do when she found him and the sex they would engage in. Ashley craved Julius at the breakfast table and she touched herself and brought her finger to his mouth and let him taste her as she stripped. She did it slowly, undoing one button at a time of the blouse she'd put on. She lowered her skirt and unhooked her bra. Then she sat on Julius's lap. She unzipped him and took out his cock. She lowered her panties and threw them on the floor then she got the handcuffs from the drawer and began to finger herself.

Ashley opened her lips and put her finger in, her eyes on Julius, a tease ready for some action. She moved slowly, the seductress now. She took him by the shirt and guided him into the living room where she lay on the floor. She put her hands on the side of the radiator.

'Cuff me,' she said.

'You really want to do this?'

'Show me. Use me as your sex toy.'

'But you're not, Ashley.'

'Not yet.'

'You want to be tied.'

'Yes, right now, do it to me right now.'

He put the cuffs around her wrists one at a time.

'Touch me,' she said.

He ran his hands across her naked body, caressed her breasts and nipples and then began to masturbate her. Ashley pulled on the cuffs, testing them, her body taut.

'Do you want me to fuck you?' Julius said.

'Yes, put it in me.'

Ashley watched as he stripped, turned on even more. He put his cock inside her and fucked her as Ashley wrapped her legs around him and pushed against him until she came. Then Julius took off her earrings, this surprised her, he did it so gently, delicately. They were a pair of gold hoops and he laid them on her nipples. He left the room, went upstairs, and returned with more of her jewellery, her emeralds and golds. He covered her naked skin with them. They were cold to the touch initially, then as Julius touched her Ashley felt expensive and desired. She wanted him to take the cuffs off and to mount him covered in jewels.

'I like it, gold on my skin,' Ashley said.

'I'll coat you in twenty-four karat if you want,' Julius said.

'This is only the beginning,' she said.

'Of Ashley's sex games.'

It surprised her how he knew, as if he could read her intentions, and yet she liked the fact that he did. Because she was halfway there to his sexual mind.

47

2:00 PM.

Tammy stared in disbelief at the pictures Karen laid on her desk. No one had ever rumbled her cover before. And yet here they were, shot after shot of her watching Micky as he observed her. She wondered what she'd done to give herself away, but could find no explanation. Karen had called her after she'd got dressed. Micky was out as she drove to Tammy's office.

'Are you sure he doesn't know you hired me?' Tammy said.

'How could he have found out?'

'Any number of ways. Do you think he listens to your calls?'

'I called you from the car.'

'Has it occurred to you that your husband may have bugged your phone?'

'If he has then he knows about everything I'm doing, including my affair.'

'It's the only explanation I can come up with.'

'If Micky knew about my affair he couldn't keep it to himself.'

'How well do you know him though? You thought he was a serial killer.'

'I know him well enough to be sure he can't have found out I'm seeing another man.'

'What if he's keeping you there for a reason?'

'Keeping me?'

'His prisoner at home, knowing all about what you do when he goes away.'

'He'd never stand for it.'

'Maybe not in the long run but he may be waiting.'

'You think he's planning to kill me.'

'If he knows about your affair he's planning something.'

'And what if he doesn't know about it?'

'How did he know he was being watched?'

'Maybe he saw you.'

'I've never been sighted when carrying out surveillance.'

'What if Gary has people making sure he's not being watched?'

'It's possible.'

48

7:00 PM.

Ashley really got turned on in the cuffs, she was in his hands, but she was directing him, telling him what to do, what moves to make. His compliance was all part of the turn on, allowing her to feel in control. Later that day she did it to him, Julius reluctant at first, then complying. She cuffed him to the bed posts. He was in his jockeys, Ashley in her bra and panties and she stripped and pulled his jockeys down.

'You know you belong to me,' she said.

'I appear to right now.'

'No I mean it. I'll treat you well but I want to find it.'

'Find what?'

'All your secret places.'

'Who says I have any?'

'I know you do, you exude sexual danger.'

She thought she would take her time, looking into his eyes, this seductress with a plan, intent on extreme pleasures. She took him in her mouth and stood over him, then lowered herself onto his cock and guided it inside her. Then she rode him, studying his face for any difference of expression to the one he usually wore when they made love. But there was none, he looked the same, even when he gave it up and she felt him throb inside her.

She lay there on him, loving the fact that he couldn't get up and was still inside her, still hard. She kissed him and began to bleed, feeling it run down her ankles to the white sheets. Ashley looked down to see what was happening, wondering if she'd begun her cycle. But that was not where the blood was coming from. She got off Julius and inspected the bed. Then she bent down to discover what had cut her as she'd leaned forward and skimmed the sheets with her foot. There beneath her leg was a single razor blade locked in her skin.

49

7:45 PM.

Ashley pulled it out and watched it drip onto the bed. Then she went into the bathroom and put a plaster on it. She was not badly hurt. But she wondered how it had got there. It was one of Julius's and as Ashley rinsed it under the tap, watching the red fade to pink, she had the overwhelming urge to take it through to the bedroom and run it across the surface of his skin to see what colour his blood was, as if she wanted him to menstruate. A bleeding Julius turned her on, she had to find his pain and then she'd have him in the way she had other men.

'Did you put it there?' she said, standing at the foot of the bed.

'The razor?'

'Did you put it on the bed? Did you want me to cut myself?'

'No of course not. I have no idea how it got there.'

'Maybe you didn't like being tied up.'

'I enjoyed it Ashley.'

'Did you? Did you really like being in my hands?'

'I thought it was a big turn on.'

She put the razor down and uncuffed him and watched him get up. And as he did she caught a sparkle in his eyes, something she had never seen before. When she looked again it was gone. And she wondered what it was, that look she saw so briefly she almost doubted she'd seen it at all.

Julius returned to his inner impenetrability, and remained endlessly seductive in his manner. And Ashley thought of ways to enter him and of extreme sexual acts.

50

Tammy told Arlene about Karen's visit as they took a long bath together. The Pimp watched it all on the new camera he'd installed in the bathroom while they were at the office. He'd taken his time, and gone through their drawers. He'd laid some new underwear in one of them.

'How do you think he found out you were watching him?' Arlene said.

'I think he's spying on his wife.'

The Pimp listened with interest and watched as Tammy stood up and rubbed soap into her breasts. Arlene got up and they lathered one another's bodies before washing and drying themselves, still talking about Micky. They took it through to the bedroom and had sex on the bed, The Pimp zooming in on them, his two dike sex kittens putting on a show for him. He'd edit it later, cutting and slicing the film of them finding pleasures. He zoomed in on their faces as they came, getting a good view of it all, liking Tammy's expression as she screamed. She'd scream for him. He'd get her to wear Holly's skirt and make her dance. He'd use his knife on them.

They were getting dressed now, Arlene putting on a pair of pink panties that showed it all, standing there with no bra on as they talked. Tammy was opening the drawer now, and The Pimp zoomed in. She was rummaging around while talking, and she pulled out a black bra and turned round. She watched as Arlene put on a pink bra and continued talking about Micky. Then she reached into the drawer and pulled it out, the leather thong he'd placed there.

'I haven't seen that before,' Arlene said.

'It's not mine, he must have put it there.'

51

Tammy stared at the thong, the smell of leather rising in the room, and she placed it on the bed and walked out into the hall. She gestured to Arlene to follow her and they went into the bathroom where she whispered they should get dressed and leave the house. They got their clothes from the bedroom, Arlene slinging on a skirt and blouse, Tammy getting into a G-string, putting on the bra she'd picked out, then a pair of jeans and a T-shirt. Then they headed out into the dark street. They talked in the car.

'He's got to have been in the house in the last twenty-four hours,' Tammy said.

'How is he getting in?'

'I don't know, and I also don't know why my cameras haven't picked him up. He must know their range and be slipping through the outside.'

'What area do they cover?'

'The front path, hall, kitchen, living room, bathroom, spare room.'

'Not the bedroom though?'

'No, he'd have to climb up to the first floor and get in, and the camera outside would catch him.'

'There are areas of the house the cameras don't scan,' Arlene said. 'He's exploiting them and we need the whole house covered.'

'I'll get onto the company.'

They talked and The Pimp listened. He had bugs in her car. He had bugs at the office. He had another gift for them and he delivered it two days later.

He came up through the floorboards by the stairs, out of the camera's range. He went upstairs and left it in the same drawer and hung the thong on the bed post.

52

Tammy received a call about The Beekeeper that day. She agreed to meet the caller, a man called Hank Adams, at her office. He arrived on time, wearing a light summer suit and sat down on the chair opposite her, leaned forwards and knitted his fingers together. He raised his clear, almost violet eyes to hers and swallowed hard, the Adams apple rising like a sharp stone in the taut skin of his throat. It was a hot day, with the temperature in the high eighties, sunlight blasted into the office through the cracks in the Venetian blinds, and Tammy could see damp patches under his arms as he reached for a tissue in his jacket pocket and dabbed at his forehead.

'Can I have a glass of water?' he said.

Tammy went and got one from the fountain in the corner of the room.

'Mr Adams, you say you have information about the killer known as The Beekeeper,' Tammy said, sitting back down again.

She watched as he sipped from the glass. He was a tall and well but man, handsome and with large hands.

'Do you want to know who he is? Do you want to know why he does what he does?'

'You know who he is?'

'Yes, I also know where you can find him. I know you track killers for a living.'

'Please tell me what you know.'

'I don't know his name, but I have seen him with his bees. I have also seen him with the body of a woman, stung to death she appeared to be, a shocking affair, one that turned my stomach inside out. It made me sick you see coming here, thinking about it. I am afraid he will do something to me if he knows. But I have to stop these women being killed.'

'Where did you see him?'

'I rented a house some weeks ago, next to an old farmhouse in the countryside. One morning I was looking out of my window when I saw this man dressed in white, the uniform of a beekeeper you see, walking across the garden next door. It has a high wall and it is impossible to see over it apart from at a particular angle of the bedroom in the cottage next door. That was where I happened to be standing. He was carrying a woman, she was naked and there were marks on her skin.'

'What sort of marks?'

'They looked like insect bites, bee stings.'

'Did you see his face?'

'Not then. He placed her in a high box, a hive, I watched the bees swarm from it. The next day I was leaving and I saw him in his front garden. I knew it was the same man.'

'How did you know that?'

'When he turned in the garden and walked back into the house he took his hat off and I caught a glint of gold in his mouth. He is a tall man of Indian descent with gold teeth.'

'This is really helpful, can you give me the address?'

'Of course that is why I have come here, so you can catch him.'

He reached out and gripped her arm.

'You have to stop him.'

'Where was the house?'

Mr Adams gave her the address in Surrey and left.

Tammy drove there that day. She went on her own, leaving Arlene to tend to a pile of paperwork at the office. She found the country lane as Hank Adams had described it, a pretty lane bordered by flowers that ended at two buildings, a cottage and a house. She got out and looked around. There were no cars parked on either drive. The cottage looked deserted.

She drew her Glock and walked up the path of the house. As she did a bee flew past her ear, the buzzing sound loud in the silent lane. She could see the front door was open. The adrenaline was pumping through her body as she put her hand on the door and pushed it an inch to peer inside, seeing only a glimpse of a darkened hallway with nothing in it except for a beekeeper's hat and some gloves. Tammy raked a bullet into the magazine and stepped into the house. She glanced up the stairs. She could see a landing at the top and two doors. There were two doors off the hallway, both closed. She tried the first door, opening it slowly, her Glock in front of her. It was a kitchen, containing a table and chair, a fridge and a sink.

She stepped back into the hall, then she heard the buzzing sound. She paused, trying to determine where it was coming from.

Then she opened the second door. There in the middle of the living room, standing on the faded carpet was a statue. She walked towards it, hearing the buzzing sound grow louder. Then she realised she was staring into the face of Dr Marjorie Tram, buried beneath wax. There was a hand written note on a small table next to her. It read, 'You really ought to eat more honey.'

Suddenly she heard a click and the wick that rose out of Dr Tram's head ignited. Then Tammy saw it, the bomb that sat between Dr Tram's thighs, a small device but one that would blow the house up. She raced out of there and down the path and got into her car as she heard the explosion. The windows were blown out and burning debris scattered across the front garden. As she started the engine she saw the swarm of bees.

They were coming out of an upstairs window. Tammy rolled up her window, turned on the air conditioning, and drove away, back to Fulham.

53

It was mailshot day for The Beekeeper. High on honey and rubber dolls, he sent a small jar to addresses across the UK, men and women he knew needed to taste his crop.

When Tammy had got back to the office she told Arlene what had happened. She'd spent the evening trying to determine which killer had lured her to the house. That morning she talked it through with Arlene. They sat in the living room drinking coffee, it was already hot outside and tammy felt sweat trickle down her back.

'If it was The Pimp then he's using The Beekeeper,' Tammy said.

'He's never involved him before,' Arlene said.

'The explosions aren't the work of The Pimp. And if he wanted to kill me I think he would abduct me first.'

'How did he get the cottage to blow up?'

'He used a remote control on the wick.'

'Then he was watching you. He knows who your doctor was, like The Pimp he's gathering information on you.'

'Why would he kill Dr Tram?'

'You get a tip off that takes you straight into a trap.'

'Mr Adams has to be The Beekeeper.'

'He wanted you to be blown up after you saw what happened to your doctor.'

'Did he target her or was she another woman with a puncture on a country road?'

As they sat there they heard the delivery and Tammy opened the box containing the honey.

In Sheen Micky received the same box and sat there at the kitchen table staring at the small jar and the liquid inside it as Karen took a shower upstairs.

Inspector Norman Hunt and Constable Harry Bright each received a jar of honey at the station where they worked. They sent them to forensics for fingerprints.

In Surrey the man who called himself Mr Adams walked up the path of a pretty cottage and knocked on the door. After a few minutes Gary Krane answered.

'I delivered a jar to the address in Sheen,' Mr Adams said.

'Marcus, how are the bees? I bet this tastes good on a set of nipples.'

'My honey always tastes good. It's because of what I feed the bees.'

'I see you have a jar for me.'

'I thought I'd bring it round, the personal touch, after that help you gave me.'

'Well, better luck next time, he's normally infallible.'

'I watched her get away, the bombs won't get her but the bees will.'

'She's been watching us too.'

Marcus handed the jar to him and Gary looked at it as the sunlight caught the gold honey beneath the glass.

'How is the midnight club?' Marcus said.

'They're good looking when they come and not so good looking when they leave.'

54

Julius went out that afternoon and Ashley began to fret after a few hours of his absence, resisting calling him, drinking a glass of wine and planning the sex. She had new ideas, ones that turned her on as she thought of doing them with him. She told herself he'd be back soon and tried to recall if he mentioned a time. Eventually she rang his mobile and got his voicemail. She left no message and retreated into her earlier sense of despair at his elusiveness and desirability, diminished by the latter, needing to reverse the former.

When he did return she tried to be distant but it didn't work, her need for him overwhelmed her resolve. She put her arms around his neck, tipsy now, and kissed him.

He offered no explanation for his absence, and she told herself why should he, she didn't expect him to stay at home all day. But she wanted one.

Over dinner she asked him, laying her fork down on the plate and staring at the pasta as it grew cold, trying to sound offhand. But her voice was strained.

'Where did you go today?' she said.

'I had some things to take care of.'

'What things? Secret things?'

'Business, Ashley.'

He held her stare and she looked away to the window and the darkened garden beyond its fractured pane. But it wasn't the glass that was broken, it was Ashley and her world of empty tricks. They didn't work with him, the one man she needed them to. And she sought her mind for the promise of reward and found only heartache and his face.

55

What it was she sought there she didn't know but she knew it existed inasmuch as the pleasure he gave her on a daily basis. But the pleasure hurt because of his remoteness. Had she angered him she thought as she got up from the table and crossed the few feet to stand by his chair. He looked up at her and she took his face in her hands and kissed his lips again.

'I get jealous, I get low,' she said.

'It won't help things.'

She lowered her skirt, naked beneath, she took his hand and placed his fingers inside her and began to rub herself with them. She undid her blouse and let it fall on his lap, noticing his hardness beneath his trousers. And they went upstairs and did it all again, and it was new with him, this inventor of sexual acts.

Afterwards she stared at his face above her, sought the man who was inside and she thought of what they would do in bed, that evening when she craved a memory. Ashley didn't know that was what she sought, she told herself she sought Julius. But the thing she needed was in the past. It lived in the other men who flickered with desire and hunger for her body.

'There are things I want do with you,' she said.

'What do you want Ashley?'

'I want to find a path there. To you.'

'I'm right here in case you didn't notice.'

'You know what I mean.'

'You should try looking away.'

Ashley turned her back and mounted him, took him all the way inside and rode him until she came. But she craved his face and looked round as she did and stared into his eyes. Her ability to scrutinise her sexual partner was lost on him, as if he could penetrate her mind and lock her out of his. Ashley wanted to enter him, but she was lost in his indigo stare.

56

Tammy had been reading Holly's letters. She and Arlene sat in the living room sharing a bottle of Pinot Grigio.

'Holly mentions that she thought this guy Julius was hiding something, but what?' Tammy said.

'She only ever spoke to me about him once.'

'And what did she say? Can you remember Arlene?'

'Yes, she said he was unlike other men, that the things men did that turned her off were lacking in him but she sensed there was something else there.'

'The letters break off at the point when she says she discovered it.'

'The Pimp has the rest,' Arlene said.

'Yes and no doubt he's saving it to shock me.'

They had some dinner and went upstairs. Tammy saw it first hanging from the bed post, a reminder from The Pimp that he could access their home any time he wanted. Arlene came in and stood behind her looking at it over her shoulder. Tammy got hold of it, took it downstairs, and slung it in the rubbish, Arlene following her.

'I called a new debugging company, they're coming tomorrow,' Tammy said.

'Do you think he's left something?'

They went back up and Tammy opened the drawer and saw it. It was a yellow bra stained with blood and with two puncture marks in the cups, where the nipples would rest. She lifted it out and held it up, examining it, trying to detach from her sense of horror and anger. But she knew whose it was before Arlene said it.

'It's Holly's. Another one of Holly's things.'

'The holes look like they were made with a knife.'

Tammy turned the bra over to study what had made the cuts and as she did something fell out of the cups. She bent and stared at the two nipples lying on the carpet. Arlene came closer and saw them too. Tammy got her latex gloves and picked them up and gently laid them back in the bra and took it downstairs. The Pimp watched as she placed it in a bag and poured herself and Arlene more wine. He listened as they talked, thinking of all the things he'd give to them both. He had a lot of Holly to place there in the house, he had a lot of her he wanted to give to them. He also had a lot he wanted to take away from them.

'He must have killed another woman,' Tammy said. 'They're not Holly's nipples.'

'Then whose are they?'

'I don't know, but these have been cut off a woman's body recently. He's sending someone else's body parts.'

'That's Holly's bra, I recognise it.'

'I know it looks like it. But it isn't hers.'

'He's kept her clothes.'

'He wants us to think that.'

'What are you going to do with them?'

The Pimp knew Tammy was trying to play a game with him, he saw through it as soon as she started it. He watched as Tammy put the items in the rubbish, on top of the thong. He'd make her wear it when he filmed her having sex with Arlene. He watched them go to bed, zooming in on their bodies as they stood there talking.

He watched Tammy climb out of bed after midnight with her Glock and go and retrieve her sister's nipples from the rubbish and sit crying in the darkened kitchen. Her face in infrared, her liquid eyes, her immediate proximity beneath the lens, her well-studied nakedness, all his. They were both his, as was Holly and the others. They were all The Pimp's whores, these well-observed woman. He showed them how to have sex, he took them to his theatre. They needed to be watched. They lived beneath the lens. Tammy stood up, wiped her eyes with the back of her hand, and aimed her Glock at the walls, scanning them for the camera. But it wasn't in the walls but in the microwave.

57

Monday 2:00 AM.

Ashley tried something new with Julius. She did it blindfolded, walking naked into the bedroom and handing it to him. He wrapped it around her face and she told him what to do, talking him through it, feeling strong even though she was at a disadvantage. The more she directed him the more she felt something new, the thing she'd sought in all the weeks of sex that left her hungry and alone, searching his face for his inner mind, the man he hid from sight with the pleasure of his touch.

'Use your fingers Julius,' she said. 'Run them across my skin and put them inside me, one by one, lead me to the bed and tether me like your sexual animal, and arouse me until I am unable to stand it any more. Kiss my mouth, yes, that's it, my nipples, and now, lick me, as I wrap my legs around your neck. Inside me now, put it in.'

It was an erotic masquerade of such intensity she came hard and fast, swollen with desire on the bed. Julius fucked her for an hour until she tore the blindfold from her eyes and climbed on top of him, riding him until he released it inside her. Then she took the blindfold and tied it around his indigo eyes. And as she did she wanted to see them, but she performed the act she thought would show her the inner man.

Ashley tried to wear him out, to erode him to the point where he would reveal the inner Julius. But she couldn't and eventually she lay on top of him. She wanted to see his eyes and as she removed the blindfold and looked at them they looked the same, unchanged. They rose from the bed and dressed and went downstairs where they drank wine in the living room. He'd done it all before, she thought as she looked at him.

'What are you trying to find?' Julius said.

'I'm trying to find you. That part you keep hidden.'

58

Karen bought a cheap pay as you go mobile phone to make her calls to Julius. She decided to stop making them in her car, wary of Micky's bugs. She waited for him to go away again, and she watched him grow more paranoid by the day. Each time he spoke to her she thought of him with Gary Krane.

'How's your fella, you seen him lately?' Micky said to her that morning over coffee.

'I haven't got a fella Micky.'

'I'll find out if you have. You know I will.'

'Look all you want, all you'll find is I go shopping, is that OK with you?'

'You think I got another woman?'

'No I don't Micky.'

'Why not?'

'I just don't think you have.'

'You saying you don't think I could get another woman?'

'No.'

'Do you want me to have another woman?'

'Micky what is wrong with you?'

'You know what's wrong with me.'

'Why don't you tell me?'

'Tell you what Karen?'

'It might help to get if off your chest.'

'I don't know what you're taking about.'

He got up from the table and went out. He was gone for hours, and Karen drove out of the area, parked in a deserted street, got out and made a call to Julius.

'I'm having to be careful,' she said, 'I think Micky has been spying on me.'

'When is he going away again?'

'I don't know, Julius. He hasn't mentioned it.'

'Maybe we should meet somewhere else.'

'Where?'

'A hotel.'

She drove home and made some lunch, a salad and cold cuts of meat. When Micky returned, Karen was in the kitchen reading a magazine. He went upstairs and packed a case, then he came back down, walked into the kitchen, and announced he was going away again, not for long, just in case she had something she wanted to do while he was gone. He stood looking down at her, waiting, his eyes on her face, as Karen carried on reading. When she said nothing he lifted the magazine out of her hands and placed it on the table, leaning forwards, both palms down, anger in his face.

'Got nothing to say Karen?'

'What is there to say?'

'When are you coming back Micky? Got something planned have you?'

'How long will you be gone?'

'Not long.'

'Well have a good trip.'

'Fancy a quick shag before I go?'

'No I don't Micky.'

'Save it for lover boy.'

'I haven't got a lover.'

'I don't believe you.'

'What makes you think I have?'

'An instinct.'

'Well you're wrong Micky.'

'Am I?'

'I'm not seeing anyone.'

'Do you think I won't find out if you are?'

'No, because there's nothing to find out.'

'You want it smeared all over you don't you?'

'What?'

'You think I'm talking about sex don't you?'

'I don't know what you're talking about.'

'Look what I got,' he said setting a plastic bag on the table with a thud.

She opened it and looked at the jar as he pulled it out and undid the lid with a loud popping sound.

'Raspberry jam, all for you Karen.'

'No.'

She stood up and inched away from him as he dipped the fingers of his right hand into the jar. Then he squeezed her throat with his other hand and knocked her head against a picture that was hanging on the wall, of a man and a woman talking in front of a shop. He smeared jam all over Karen's mouth and poked his fingers in, touching her teeth then her gums as she struggled with him. A blue vein throbbed on her neck and as Micky looked at it he became excited and aroused and began to kiss her. Karen bit his lip and he pushed her hard against the picture. Then he pulled away and watched as Karen wiped the jam from her lips. But the picture was cracked and Micky stared at the break in the glass. Karen put her hand to the back of her head and removed a shard of glass from her skull.

'Do you know what they're talking about in that picture?' Micky said.

'I'm bleeding.'

'You can't bleed, remember. He's telling her he can see what she does.'

'Micky let me go to the bathroom.'

'I see what you do. I live in the glass of your mind.'

'It's your mind that is made of glass, it's cracked.'

'You talk about honey, I talk about jam.'

'You see bees Micky, you see bees in mouths and you need to violate.'

'You want to wash it away don't you?'

'I need to stop the blood.'

'But you can't, can you?'

'If you'll get out of my way.'

'Your seeds are gone, no children for Karen Sincere, only lovers.'

'I haven't got any lovers.'

'Where do you think I got my name?'

'What?'

'I stole it from you, there is no sincerity here any more, only lies and spies, we live in a camera.'

'What you did to me the other day when I got out of the shower.'

'What about it Karen?'

'I didn't send the jar of honey.'

'Who did then?'

'I don't know'

'Why would someone send it here?'

'You came in and choked me, your hand was covered in the stuff.'

'I thought you'd like it, since you don't like my jam.'

'What have you done with it?'

'It's here Karen, look.'

He opened a cupboard and removed The Beekeeper's jar of honey and then smashed it on the floor. Lifting a shard of glass out of it he opened his shirt and cut himself.

'No bee lives in my blood but only the sweet things I want to have on my skin. I bet this turns you on.'

'No it does not turn me on.'

She brushed past him and went upstairs, and Micky followed. He stood by the bathroom sink and watched as she applied a tissue to the cut. And she looked at him in the mirror and he returned her gaze, his eyes absent, wandered, as if he dwelt somewhere else. Karen turned on the tap and wiped the jam from her lips and watched it run down the sink.

'You would never coat my mouth with honey,' Karen said.

'You're coated in seeds now.'

'If you tried to rub honey into my lips you would remember the boy's face. It's true isn't it Micky, you're avoiding the bees.'

'I like jam, Karen, I like the taste of it.'

'You never eat jam, you just rub it into my lips.'

'I have it every day for breakfast.'

'No, you have a fry up Micky.'

'I never eat fried food, just jam.'

'And honey.'

'No.'

'Honey Micky, made by bees, the ones inside your head.'

'Do you know they're made of rubber?'

'What are?'

'Bees, like the latex you make me wrap around my penis so you can pretend you're fertile.'

'You never wear a condom.'

'You like to slide it down the shaft, makes you feel horny doesn't it?'

'You force it inside me, there is no rubber involved at all.'

'Rubber with wings on it, that's how they make all the jam, because the condoms burst, you see, and the honey drips through the tear like liquid sugar, like semen in the rain.'

'You've never once offered me protection in bed, even when we first met all those years ago.'

'The dogs protect you, they're not made of rubber.'

'Those dogs are there to scare me.'

'Have you been feeding them honey again?'

'I hate feeding them.'

'Meat Karen, give them raw meat.'

'I thought you were going on a trip.'

'I am.'

'Well then?'

'I know what you want.'

'What?'

'You want to build a beehive.'

'Why would I want to do that?'

'Because you think of stinging me with a stiletto heel coated in your menses.'

He stood there nodding and then he walked away. Karen waited as she heard the front door close and his car start up and fade. Then she went downstairs to the kitchen and cleaned up the jam on the floor, tipping the seeds into the dustbin. As she did she saw The Times lying inside it, it was open at a page that showed a picture of Gary Krane. She pulled it out and read an article that described how another businessman had been shot. He was competing with Gary Krane over a company takeover. On the next page was an article about the plight of the honey bee. Ash from one of Micky's cigars lay scattered across it like charred and hollowed wood and as she put the paper down it rose from the surface as if it had wings and was trying to find a way out of the house and its world of surveillance and menace and it hovered in the air like feathers torn from a bird.

59

The company came to Tammy's house that day, swept for cameras and found only two, one in the bedroom lodged in a picture, the other in the bathroom in a cupboard. The Pimp had been able to disguise them so well that even the experts missed the remaining ones, in the kitchen and the living room, another in the bedroom and bathroom. They added cameras to cover the entire house, including the hallway by the stairs. As soon as they were gone The Pimp hacked the camera by the stairs using remote access. He would turn it away from the area it covered when he wanted to leave gifts for his two whores.

'Now we have some privacy,' Tammy said to Arlene.

'For how long though?'

'I'll know if he gets in. The whole house is on film.'

'He's still following us.'

The Pimp listened to them talk about ways of eluding and catching him. When they went to the office he watched them go inside, sitting in a white van parked at the end of the street. He turned the cameras in the hallways and the bedroom round before he got to the house, coming up through the floorboards. He went into the bedroom and he laid it on the bed, the first part of the film. It was in a box and on CD.

The Pimp also placed several items of lingerie in the bedroom, placing them neatly on a chair, items he was going to get them to wear. Then he left the way he came in. Several screws were missing from two boards. He'd taken them out when he first started visiting them. He had them at his cinema, and he thought of uses for them, of driving them through Holly's tongue.

When Tammy and Arlene got home they found the box and put the CD in the player downstairs in the living room. And they stared at themselves having sex in The Pimp's film.

60

Micky and Gary Krane were having a beer that evening at Gary's house. It was a neat cottage in the Surrey countryside, more fitting to a retired school teacher than a gangland killer. Bur Gary had done it up to look like the interior of a wealthy London home, removing many of the original effects of the cottage. He'd put in down lighting and filled it with a collection of bizarre and tasteless furniture. A huge pink sofa filled the living room. Pictures of naked women adorned the walls, strangely, since he despised the female body.

'She doesn't suspect a thing,' Micky said.

'She sent the detective. She'll have seen the pictures she took.'

'I've told her I think it's business. And she believes me.'

'Is she that dumb?'

'Scared.'

'Of what?'

'Me knowing.'

'Scared of what you'll do.'

'To her and lover boy.'

'And what would you do?'

'What do you fucking think?'

'Good looking fella is he?'

Micky nodded.

Gary Krane sipped his beer. He was a handsome man with eyes that flickered with predatory thoughts.

'Why do you have those on the wall?' Micky said, pointing at a picture of a nude woman.

'Because that's all they're good for, taking their clothes off.'

'Like looking at them do you?'

'What do you think?'

'I think you don't like women.'

'Porn. I like them in porn, it's like watching a comedy to me, and I like a good laugh.'

'You remind me of someone,' Micky said.

'Yeah, and who's that?'

'Someone I knew long ago.'

'A lover?'

'No, I was too young for all that.'

'Want another beer Micky?' Gary said, going to the bar at the end of the room and holding up a bottle of Heineken.

But Micky didn't hear him, he was gazing out of the window at a beehive at the far end of the garden.

'Every time I see that, I think of him,' he said.

'You on about them bees again?'

'It's the buzzing sound they make.'

'Yeah, that's what bees do. They buzz.'

'Have you ever heard what they sound like inside a mouth, a human mouth?'

'No I ain't, as a matter of fact,' Gary said, snapping the top off a bottle.

'Why did you put it there?' Micky said.

Gary put the bottle to his mouth and tilted it.

'Because that's what the fuckers in the countryside do.'

'All part of your country gent image, hah?' Micky said, turning round.

'That's right.'

'How's business?'

'We got more competition on the prostitution front, a couple of wide boys from the East End.'

'Trouble?'

'Nothing I can't handle, but they have security, good security.'

'What are you gonna do?'

'I think I'll use Hundred Percent on this one.'

'He's that good ain't he?'

'Never fails. You ever met him?'

'No.'

'Thought not, well, no need to is there?'

Tammy sat outside their house and took some shots that evening as the sun set. She took one of Micky kissing Gary and of Gary getting undressed in the bedroom. They had her in their sights as well, and got her number plate, running it through their system and finding out where she lived. They knew all about Tammy by the time she got home.

61

That evening Inspector Norman Hunt was called out to Herbert Reed's address. A neighbour had reported a violent commotion. Constable Harry Bright was away on a short break fishing in the Surrey countryside and Hunt went there with another officer who was suffering from a head cold. Hunt parked the car opposite the flat of the man he suspected had killed Joyce Farmer and radioed for backup. Despite numerous attempts to locate Reed, Hunt had not managed to find out his whereabouts. And the longer that had gone on the more he became convinced that Reed had fled the country. Hunt glanced at the address, seeing the front door was open. Now was his chance to arrest Reed and show Tammy Wayne that there was no such killer as The Pimp. The media had a good story, all right.

'Dear oh dear, you look a mess,' Hunt said to his colleague, 'stay here.'

He got out of the car, drew his taser and peered into the hallway. As he did he heard the noise of a swarm of bees. Hunt began to back down the path. Then the explosions went off. His colleague watched as the front windows were blown out and Hunt was thrown back into the street. He clambered out of the car as the backup arrived.

They called for an ambulance and rushed Hunt to hospital. From the inside of an old van parked at the end of the road The Beekeeper watched as Hunt was blown up.

It was too late for Hunt, and the fire brigade took several hours to put out the smouldering building. The neighbours were out at the time. When the police spoke to them both sides claimed they had not made a call, nor had they heard a disturbance. They said they hadn't seen the owner for days.

Meanwhile Constable Bright was having a good time. He hadn't seen the man watching him from the van earlier that day as it idled on the road near to where he fished.

62

That evening Ashley and Julius ate at home, Ashley more watchful now of going out, as if she didn't want other women's eyes on him. She put on a designer skirt, one she'd modelled in and a blue blouse. She made pasta and salad and they drank wine. And she talked to him about her sexual desires.

'I want us go further in bed,' she said.

'What are you saying?'

'I want to explore every part of it with you. I've never done these things before.'

'How far do you want to go?'

'Until I find you.'

'I'm right here Ashley.'

'There's something you're holding back.'

'I'm not.'

'You know right now, I'm touching myself, I'm not wearing any panties.'

'Do you want me to fuck you on the kitchen table?'

'Yes, do it now.'

Ashley stood up and lifted her skirt. She was wet and continued to rub herself as she moved the plates and cutlery to clear a space for them. Then she lay back and Julius unzipped his fly and began to lick her. There among the wine and the supper he entered her and fucked her until she came.

Julius came hard and strong inside her and she caught a flicker of something else in his eyes as he did. She was getting there.

63

Ashley was getting hooked on the acts she'd never done before, all of them, all the discreet erotic surprises her mind began to offer her on a reel of film. She performed an act of such extreme arousal that Julius showed a side to his passion she hadn't seen before. They were in the living room when she got out the chains. She held them to the light, watched the links sparkle, saw her face in their hard metal, and began to strip, then got down on her hands and knees, thighs apart showing it all.

'I'm going to be your sex slave, Julius, show me how you'd treat me if you had me in chains,' she said.

She moaned as he rose from the sofa and complied, ever the graceful lover, attendant to her desires.

Julius wrapped the chains around her ankles, not too tight, but enough to make it real, then the other end around her wrists. Ashley's eyes were raised, she looked like an animal on heat as Julius stripped and stood over her, erect, priapic. He bent and took her mouth to his and Ashley thrust her tongue in. Then Julius slid his cock in.

Ashley pushed back against him with her tight buttocks, enjoying the ride as he pumped her hard and she felt him come. So this was a turn on to him, to have her captive. But why she wondered, when she already was in so many ways. She wondered if it was her physical imprisonment he craved.

'Do you want me to untie you so you can do it to me Ashley, do you want to be the mistress of my cock?' Julius said.

She did and he removed the chains and let them fall to the floor. Then Ashley shackled him to the sofa and took charge of ecstasy.

64

11:30 PM.

As she moved on him and took him deep inside she gauged his eyes for surrender. She needed him to yield to her female desire, to be her captive for an hour. She needed his compliance in her sin, his endless unfolding there beneath her skin. Ashley needed Julius to be her sexual toy, a living dildo she'd enjoy.

'Do you know what I'm going to do to you?' Ashley said, speaking low, almost a whisper, her mouth pressed to Julius's ear.

'I know what you're doing. What you're doing right now.'

'No, what I'm going to do to you while I have you like this? What you secretly desire.'

'Tell me.'

'I'm going to show you, open your mouth and take them in.'

She leaned forwards and put one nipple in his mouth and Julius sucked on it as Ashley clenched her cunt around the shaft of his throbbing cock and took his balls in her other hand, seeking semen. She rode him hard and changed breasts, thrusting her other nipple past his lips as his tongue licked it and Julius began to come hard and strong inside her.

As he did Ashley stared into his eyes and saw herself there etched forever on the tide of sex, but she thought she saw a flicker of another man, one whose face bore the remnants of a life of cruelty. And it tormented her and she hungered to tame him, to anchor him to her body with sex games she planned at midnight as he slept, her finger inside her. Licking the sweat away she got off Julius and touched his cock, squeezing it hard and daring him to get harder.

'Do you think you can do it?' Ashley said.

'All the way to your sexual core.'

65

11:45 PM.

It surprised her when he said it, as if he'd stolen the words from her mind and inhabited her like an erotic deity. But he was inside her every day. She was scared too, and wondered how he knew what she thought. He was a sexual mind reader and he was immersed in the body of her desire.

They went upstairs and slept. The next morning Julius entered her on the bed, Ashley lying on the white sheets that caught the sunlight filtering through the trees outside and turned their pattern into lace. He fucked her slowly and then harder as she came and pulled him towards her, searching his face as he held her gaze.

Ashley's sexual game had only just begun, and she thought of many things they would do. She wanted to do them all with him.

The craving was there and it held her in its hands as her body found new arousals that day and Julius found a way of keeping her in orgasm. She rode the wave of burning ecstasy.

'Come over to the window,' Julius said.

'Do you want me facing the garden?'

He showed her with his hands, touching her breasts as he opened the window and turned her around. Then Ashley laid her hands on the sill and leaned forwards, pushing her buttocks against him as he plunged his cock in. Julius took both her breasts in his hands as he pushed hard. And Ashley came again.

But the orgasm went on and on, Julius fucking her still, Ashley weak from pleasure, dripping and crackling with arousal. It continued for an hour or more in which she melted. And what it was she melted into was the woman on the catwalk, a body of beauty endlessly arousing to the eyes of watchful men intent on seductions. Ashley was erotic liquid.

He washed her then, took her into the bathroom and stood her beneath a hot shower, rubbing soap into her nipples. Julius washed away the ache. Ashley hadn't seen the man she knew lived there in his mind, but she sensed she was nearing the time when he would open up to her. She devised new ways. They dressed at one o'clock and went out to eat and she saw the women look and stare at the man who seduced them all in private places among the lost and broken moments of their lives, so Ashley thought. But he was hers and she felt aroused, sitting there, beautiful at the table set with sparkling cutlery and a bottle of red wine.

'Take me home and fuck me,' she said.

'There is nothing I want more.'

Ashley said it loud enough for the waiter to hear. Loud enough for people at the next table to turn their heads and stare, and she wanted to do it there in front of them, to show them what she had. She pictured herself on the table, her legs astride Julius's waist, and him inside her all the way to the dessert menu. She would taste them all, all the hidden pleasures from the slick and polished trolley of pleasures. She wanted it pink and sugared, dripping with honey, alive with the sound of long midnight moans.

She wanted it long and hard burnt like vanilla, soft like a sugared fondue, melting like bees' wax and dissolving like candyfloss on her lapping tongue. She thought of all the things she wanted him to do to her there among the watchful distant diners. For their distance was their lack of pleasure and the pleasure was all hers. He took her back to her flat and did them all, knowing her needs, raising her threshold as she came again. He did them all.

66

Tammy and Arlene played it again late that night, watched the film and The Pimp's depiction of their sex acts knowing they did the things it showed, but not in that way.

'He's been filming us for weeks,' Tammy said.

'He's seen it all, everything we've done. And he's changed it.'

'I wonder what else he's got on film. And how he got in the house.'

'There's nothing on the CCTV cameras.'

'He must have hacked them.'

'Which means he saw them installing them.'

The Pimp listened as they talked, amused by all this. Then Tammy and Arlene left the house and walked to the end of the road.

'He's controlling our surveillance system,' Tammy said.

'He must get in while we're at the office.'

'We stay there for long enough to make him watch us there. We spot his vehicle.'

'And in the meantime we don't have sex?

'No, we have sex but not at home.'

'How do we know he hasn't got access to the cameras at the office?'

'We don't.'

'Then he'll know what we're doing.'

'I'm taking them down.'

67

They did it first thing, removing all the cameras from the office, feeling bare without them but naked with them and The Pimp inhabiting their lenses like a silent spy. Tammy wondered briefly whether she was giving him what he wanted, an ease of access without any threat of detection, but then he was manipulating the show and had been all along. If he wanted to get in he would do it any way. At least this way when they spoke they would do so undetected. But what about at home, she thought. They were unwatched at the office but he had violated her house, her sister, and Arlene, and now he was violating her mind.

She made some coffee and considered that now began the long wait for him. These would be days of constant watchfulness on her part, full of furtive glances from the window at cars in the street below, of the checking of rear view mirrors all the way from home to office. Tammy knew it wouldn't be easy, The Pimp evaded detection better than anyone, but if he was following them she would eventually spot him and get his number plate. That morning she drove round to Sheen to continue her surveillance of Micky. His car was gone and she put a call through to Karen.

'Has he said anything?' she said.

'Only that he thinks I've got a lover.'

'I think he knows. Have you been followed?'

'The other week a man was outside my lover's flat.'

'Then Micky has you under surveillance.'

'My boyfriend said it was to do with him, he owes money to someone.'

'Are you sure it's not Micky?'

'He went down and spoke to the man.'

'Then Micky must have found out through some other means.'

'He must have bugged me.'

'You ought to warn your boyfriend.'

'I will, I'm seeing him today.'

As Tammy returned to the office a white van almost knocked her of the road. When she got to the office Arlene was gone and her blood stained skirt was on her desk.

68

2:00 PM.

Karen went to see Julius while Micky was out, taking a different route to his flat, parking some streets away. Ashley was on a model shoot. It was too late to arrange a room at a hotel and so Karen went there, checking her rear view mirror all the way. The heat was rising again, as if a second summer was on its way, after recent days of rain. They sat in the living room, Karen anxious that what she was about to say would drive Julius away.

'I need to warn you about Micky,' she said.

'You think he knows?'

'I think he's listened to my calls. I also know he'll want to hurt you.'

'Is he away at the moment?'

'Yes, with his boyfriend Gary.'

'Did you see anyone following you?'

'No.'

'If either of them come after me I'll take care of them.'

'Julius, you're a lover, they're dangerous.'

'I can handle myself.'

'Do you think you can handle me for an hour?'

They went into the bedroom and he took her all the way to that high and lingering ecstasy that felt like erotic wine coursing through her veins. And as Karen came she resolved she'd be rid of Micky. She didn't have much time that day and so she took from Julius what she needed and returned home to her emptiness and broken life with a man who allowed her no rest, and whose immoral compulsions and sexual dishonesty had eroded more of her than she wanted to consider.

The day crawled past the window like a silent film. She watched others' lives from the living room, seeing women laughing in the street outside beneath a burning blue sky that spoke of summer, flowers in bloom, of the fertile things, while she remained locked in the sterile house with the dogs outside. She watched these figures pass by, briefly visible beyond the gate. She went into the garden and drank wine, waiting for his return. But it didn't come. There was no Micky there that evening, and she phoned Julius again and arranged to meet him. And Julius calculated ways to do it under the watchful eyes of Ashley.

\#

Tammy and Arlene were having coffee at the office.

'I thought he'd taken you,' Tammy said.

'The skirt must have been a shock. I guess it's the stress, knocking the glass over.'

'Do you want me to take another look at the cut on your hand?'

'It's OK, I saw this van outside and was convinced it was him.'

'I saw it too.'

'My hand slipped on the broken glass. I took my skirt off and went to the bathroom.'

'I think it was The Pimp in the van, I think he is going to abduct us.'

69

Constable Harry Bright had stayed on an extra day for his break. He caught fish, cooked them on an outside barbecue, and drank too much. And he forgot about his job and the tedium it involved for him. For on a daily basis Bright felt his work involved catching criminals less and less and instead more and more dull paperwork. He received the call about Hunt the day before he left. He packed early, and drove straight to the station.

Bright was convinced they were onto Reed, and that he had set Hunt up. That afternoon he met with his senior officer.

Bright told him about the visit to Reed's flat and his disappearance, he told him about their visit to Tammy Wayne. His superior officer asked him why Reed would risk an arson charge if they had nothing firm on him. Bright replied that there were no other suspects in the murder of Joyce Farmer. When The Pimp was mentioned Bright stated that he saw no evidence for his existence.

He spent the rest of the day at his desk doing paperwork, thinking about his holiday and how to catch Reed. When he left to go home he didn't see the van follow him.

Bright entered his newly built house and turned off the alarm. He opened a can of beer and sat and thought about the case.

Then he heard the noise of the buzzing of bees. It sounded as though it was coming from the hall and Bright went to investigate.

As he did two explosions ripped through his house. The front of the house was blown across the road and Bright was thrown against the wall.

When the ambulance arrived there was nothing the paramedics could do for Bright. They waited for the fire brigade as the van at the end of the road drove away.

70

Friday 12:00 AM.

They called it the midnight club and it belonged to them. They used booze and drugs and they polished the knives before the blood was shed. They liked them young, guys in their twenties, guys who worked out, had a fake tan, earrings, guys who dressed like gays. Gary and Micky always dressed straight especially when they entertained them. They did the sex first over at the cottage in what Gary called his fuck room, a bare place full of stains and memories that consoled him in his frequent and vindictive rages. He dwelt between release and anticipation like a tense muscle. Micky and Gary took it in turns with the guys, then they took them out into the fields beyond his property, right up to the perimeter fence of barbed wire and rotting wood. It was a procedure Micky new well, a little cutting, a little sadism and the guys got sent home with pockets full of cash. But this night something happened, something that took Micky back to the scarred past and the small boy who existed inside him like a bruise. Gary had been getting increasingly angry at the surveillance he knew he was under, making dark threats to do things to Tammy. When the guys arrived he was rougher than usual, and there was a look in his eyes Micky did not like at all. He thought of Karen and consoled himself with the rage he exerted on her body in their bedroom. After the sex that did little to arouse Micky, that made his question his relationship with Gary and left his head full of a swarming sound, they went out into the black fields. The guys were laughing, sipping beer, spilling it, and Gary stood there like a statute, unmoving. To Micky, the trees looked like knots rising from the earth.

There beneath a silver moon whose light made Gary's eyes look like steel balls in his face, Micky saw his expression change from the look of pleasure that he carried away from the sex to a hatred that make Micky's heart race. Gary pulled a knife from his belt and moved towards one of the guys, then he slashed his throat. It was a deep hard cut that severed the carotid artery. The other guy started screaming. Gary's face was spattered with blood. He turned to Micky with feral eyes, and grinned, his teeth like metal spikes in his tight mouth, like the sharpened prong on the belt that Micky gripped, cutting his thumb on it as he watched Gary drag the other guy into some bushes and stab him, leaning down into his work, the blade tearing the flesh, a harsh staccato noise in the silent night. Micky looked on, hearing bees swarm through the woods like a cloud full of guilt and pain. Gary stopped. He lifted his head and looked at Micky, the knife dripping in his hand.

'Why did you do it Gary?' Micky said.

'Why do you think?'

'Normally it's just cutting. That's enough blood for the turn on you like.'

'How do you know what I like?'

They buried them in silence, labouring into the night with shovels. The sound of their blades slicing the earth made Micky think of fabric tearing. He saw the face of the boy he killed with bees. He recalled how he tore apart the leather gloves he'd worn to reach into his mouth. He remembered how he cut them and tore them to shreds and the sound they made that day he buried it all. Karen was right, he thought. And Gary looked just like the boy. It was getting light when they went back into the cottage. Micky drank some vodka, neat, hit after hit, feeling it work its way into his belly as he tried to reassert his stance in front of Gary. The postures he adopted, the tough guy routine he played for Karen worked well enough to dispel the bitter memory of the scene that had made his stomach knot and filled him with a feeling he found hard to name but which made him need to touch a woman in the way he liked to touch a woman. What Micky felt was fear, but he didn't know it. Karen would take it away, he'd stuff her stockings in her mouth.

He looked at Gary as he talked about business, as detached form the events that had occurred as if it was all a film on his plasma screen. They lay in the Jacuzzi and sipped from Heineken bottles and talked about what they were going to do to Karen and her boyfriend. And Micky drifted from the murder to thinking about how he would regain himself, the man who collected knives and hated his own nipples. Gary came up with an idea that Micky liked.

'What we do is we make them fuck in front of us, say if they do it good enough they get away,' Gary said.

'And what if they do it good enough?'

'We kill them anyway. Who do you want to take out first?'

'Lover boy.'

'Makes sense.'

'I want to take my time with Karen.'

'I saw Marcus the other day.'

'What he came here?'

'Brought me some honey.'

'Marcus and his bees.'

'Did you get a jar of honey on the post?'

'I did as a matter of fact,' Micky said, sitting up, and watching water drip from his scarred nipples.

'I think he sent it.'

'Why would he do that?'

'Because he wants people to taste his honey.'

'How did he get my address?'

'The midnight club belongs to us.'

'Good thing he wasn't here tonight.'

'He stopped coming a while ago, and I don't think he'd care about the killing.'

'What makes you say that?'

'I think he's The Beekeeper.'

'How many killers do you know Gary?'

'I guess it's time for you to go,' Gary said, looking out of the window at the sun and an azure sky that looked like blue ink on the horizon.

Micky got dressed and drove back to London. He entered a darkened house and climbed the stairs thinking about his conversation with Gary.

The bedroom was dark and Karen was asleep but it didn't stop him putting on the lights and dragging the sheets off her and raping her, one hand over her mouth. But as he reclaimed his heterosexual property, he lost all pleasure in the act and stood up sharply at the end and walked away. He went downstairs to the kitchen where he drank a whisky as Karen came up behind him with a kitchen knife. Micky turned and grabbed her wrist, wrestling the knife from her hand. He put it on the counter and wagged a finger at her.

'If you want to knife me in the back you'll have to be quicker than that.'

'I want to leave you Micky.'

'You want me to show you how to use a knife Karen?'

'No.'

'It's time you got out of bed anyway.'

'You stumble into the house and wake me and do that to me.'

'You're my wife aren't you?'

'No, I'm another dog in chains.'

'Do you want some raw meat in your mouth, is that what you want Karen?'

'Feed them.'

'I'll feed them when I feel like it.'

'You haven't fed them in days Micky, they're becoming savage.'

'Why don't you do it?'

'Because they scare me.'

'You want to go to lover boy.'

'I want to get out of this house.'

'You think it's that easy don't you?'

'No I don't think it's easy Micky.'

'Someone's spying on me.'

'Like you spy on me.'

'I think it's you.'

'I'm going to take a shower.'

'Washing ain't going to change it Karen.'

She went upstairs and Micky followed. He stood in the bedroom as she turned on the shower and he listened to the hiss of the water. He lit a panatela and smoked it in the bedroom, where he knew she hated him to smoke, then he went and looked out of the window at the back garden. He could see his neighbour in the next garden dressed in a white suite, his head covered. Micky took the cigar out of his mouth. His neighbour was walking towards a beehive. Micky stared at his gloved hands as he opened the lid. The scene was hazy as Micky watched through the smoke that rose from the burning tip of his cigar. Then the bees began to swarm out and Micky tasted honey beneath the tobacco.

71

Ashley wore silk stockings that morning, nothing else, as she rode Julius in their sunlit bedroom. She felt, more and more, with each new sexual performance that she was gaining on the inner man. She could sense him and his desires. Ashley the seductress, Julius beneath her, her erotic male ecstasy, priapic and unknowable. But she would know him.

'Do you like the things I do to you in bed?' she said over breakfast.

'You know I do.'

'I'm introducing all sorts of things into the bedroom. I wonder if they'll fit.'

'You make it sound like furniture.'

'Hm, that can be arranged.'

'What?'

'I want you to penetrate me in other ways.'

'There are many forms of ecstasy.'

'And I want to penetrate you, Julius.'

'Physically hard for a woman to do.'

'I'm not talking about that or implements.'

'You're talking about the mind.'

'I am.'
'I may have to slip out this afternoon.'
'Now why doesn't that surprise me?'

72

Karen dried her eyes in the bathroom, then applied mascara. She'd heard Micky's Bentley crunch the gravel on the drive earlier and now she left to meet Julius. She saw no cars tailing her, but still she parked in another road and walked to the flat. She told Julius what Micky had done.

'He raped you Karen,' Julius said.

'It's not the first time he's done it.'

'Do you think he knows about me? Or is he bluffing?'

'I think he knows.'

'I'm not scared of Micky.'

'Julius you can't mess with him,' she said.

'If he attacks me what am I meant to do?'

'Then there's Gary who's had people killed. What can you do against him?'

'I'm not just going to let them attack me.'

'You know you've never once said you regretted meeting me.'

'Because I don't Karen.'

'He watches me, watches every move I make, waits for signs of infidelity.'

'What does your private investigator think?'

'She says he's onto her.'

'He spotted her fast. I thought you said she was good.'

'She is. Tammy Wayne is meant to be the best.'

'Why did you hire her?'

'I read about her in the papers.'

'So have I and she sounds messed up.'

'What, because of her sister?'

'She's not a professional.'

'Why do you say that?'

'She's obsessed with a killer called The Pimp.'

'It doesn't stop her being effective.'

'She wasn't effective with you.'

'Micky's a hard one to catch.'

'Maybe he paid her. Maybe he knew you'd hired her.'

Karen looked at Julius and he seemed deeply troubled. She told herself it was hearing about Micky and the things he did. She told herself she was soiled by her husband and his gay lover and Julius was afraid of them. She thought of Micky waiting for her at home and she got her coat and prepared to leave.

73

11:00 AM.

Ashley was outside as Karen stepped out into the street. Ashley followed her home and watched her enter her house. Then she returned to her flat and waited for Julius. He didn't get back until after midnight and when he did she simply went to bed and waited for him.

'How was your visit to the flat?' she said as she felt him get under the sheets.

'All right.'

'Meet anyone? Do anything?'

'A friend came round, we had a chat.'

'She looked nice, did you fuck her?'

Julius turned the light on and sat up, looking down at Ashley. She searched his eyes for anger but saw only a latent curiosity.

'When are you going to stop being so jealous?'

'When you stop fucking other women.'

'I thought you were at a model shoot. Have you been following me?'

'I watched her leave, she looked like she'd been seen to, by you.'

'What did she look like?'

Ashley described her, and watched as Julius looked away. It was the first time she'd caught him off guard and she felt strangely aroused by it. She touched him, she felt her hunger grow. Then she pulled back the sheets and got on top of him, staring down into his eyes.

Ashley's body was awash with moonlight as it drifted through the parted curtains, her legs astride Julius and she felt she was dominating him. She knew what she would say and how she'd push away the anger she'd instilled in him, so well hidden but there, she could feel it in his muscles.

'You say you didn't fuck her,' she said afterwards, still on top of him.

'I didn't.'

'All right. I went round there to find you, I was a little thrown when I saw her leave.'

'You've nothing to worry about, she's my sister.'

'Will you let me meet her?'

'I don't see why not.'

The next morning they ate breakfast together and talked about going away for a short trip somewhere hot. Ashley wanted him to make love to her on a deserted beach. She wanted his body in all sorts of exotic situations that ran through her mind like an erotic film. And she wanted Julius in chains as she aroused him endlessly naked and alone.

At noon he left to do some errands and Ashley drove round to the house she'd seen the woman enter when she followed her. She sat there and waited and after an hour she saw her leave and get into her car. She tailed her to a street where she watched as the woman got out and made a call on her mobile phone as she walked along the pavement. Ashley came up behind her as she said

Julius's name. She heard enough to know he was lying. As the woman ended the call Ashley hit her hard enough to knock her over. She grabbed fistfuls of hair with her nails and tore her blouse and a passing motorist called the police.

74

It was quite a day. Karen got home with a few scratches but badly shaken by the attack, not knowing who she was, thinking Micky was behind it, thinking no. She was pouring herself a glass of Sauvignon Blanc when she heard Micky come in. He walked into the kitchen and took the bottle she was holding from her hand.

'What you up to?' he said.

'I'm having a drink, what does it look like?'

'It looks like you've been in a cat fight. And they're always over a guy Karen.'

'I fell into a rose bush.'

'There aren't any rose bushes in our garden.'

'It wasn't in our garden.'

'Those are the scratch marks made by a woman's hands.'

'I have not been fighting.'

'You think you can lie to me? Are you that dumb?'

'I'm not lying to you.'

'Yeah?'

'What's put it into your head I'm seeing someone?'

'You have.'
'How?'
'By the way you're acting.'
'I'm not acting any differently.'
'I'm gonna go and see him.'
'Who?'
'Julius.'
'Who's he?'
'Lover boy.'

75

'I don't have a lover Micky, do you?'

'What's that supposed to mean?'

She was about to answer him when he grabbed her wrist and a dragged her upstairs. He took her into the spare room and opened the cupboard full of knives, a glint in his eyes. Karen stood there as Micky pulled one out, a slender knife with a sharp tip. He held it up to her face.

'These are the things I do for you,' he said.

'You don't do them for me, Micky.'

He unbuttoned his shirt and cut off his nipples. Then he tried to force them down Karen's throat but she ran from him. He caught her in the hall, blood weeping down his chest. He had both nipples in his other hand and he held it out, palm upwards and looked down at them.

'I am not a woman, I do not need them.'

'Are you afraid you are gay?'

He let them drop to the floor and watched them settle on the carpet. Then he looked at Karen and lifted her skirt until her panties were showing.

'Have you any honey in there?' he said.

'No I am not a hive.'

'But you're shaped like one.'

'You think sex with a woman is like entering a swarm of bees.'

Micky went to the bathroom. That's when Karen left the house. She drove straight to Julius's flat but he wasn't there. And so she called him just as Ashley walked through the door. Ashley heard the conversation, standing at the end of the hallway, Julius in the kitchen. She heard him say her name. She went into the kitchen as Julius was getting off the phone.

'I need to go out,' he said.

'To Karen?'

'Was it you who attacked her? Are you that obsessed?'

'A man like you instils obsession in a woman's heart.'

'I have to go out. I wondered where you'd been.'

'Giving my version to the cops.'

'I'll ask her not to press charges if it helps.'

'Helps? What, me with my jealousy while you go off and fuck her?'

'Look I've got to go.'

'To her.'

'To my flat.'

And so he did, walking out of the door as Ashley stared after him. He got a taxi to Kew where Karen was waiting for him outside.

Micky was sitting in his Bentley at the end of the road watching him, and Julius saw the car, figured it was him. He and Karen went upstairs.

76

4:30 PM.

As Karen remembered it later, it all happened fast. They were in the living room talking, when they heard the door being kicked in downstairs.

Julius got up from his chair as Micky entered the room with a butcher's knife. He had that look in his eyes Karen knew too well, the stare of the savage man finally loosed from his chains, and he looked just like the dogs at the back of the house. He stopped and stared at Julius. The two men said nothing, simply exchanged the glances of rivals, and for the first time Karen saw anger in Julius's eyes. Then Micky advanced on him with the knife. Julius whipped his fist into Micky's head and knocked him to the floor. Then he pulled the knife from his hand.

'You really gonna use that thing?' Micky said, getting up.

'I have no intention of buggering you with it.'

'Funny guy. You won't be for much longer.'

'I thought that's what you liked, homoerotic violence.'

'I'm gonna come back with my dogs and feed you to them,' Micky said.

'I suggest you go home before I hurt you,' Julius said.

'You're coming with me Karen, now.'

'No she's not, go and play with your pets.'

Karen was surprised when Micky left. He drove home to Sheen thinking of the dogs and what he would do with them, how they would sink their canines into Julius's bones and he would watch and drag Karen back. He'd drag her back by her hair if he needed to, through the streets. Then he felt a fist twisting against his scalp, a hand in his hair and the voice of reprimand. He recalled the punishment he received when he was caught stealing jam from the larder. He recalled being a boy who lived with a mute mother and the stern nanny who reprimanded him. He recalled his taste for jam and the little he was allowed to spread on his bread. And he began to shrink inside his own skin. He relived the silence of his mother's world and the lack of maternal connection, and he saw his nanny twist his hair and scold him.

Micky made a call to Gary. Then he got out of his Bentley and walked across the drive, but he did not hear the gravel crunch beneath the soles of his shoes. He entered the kitchen and took off his jacket. Two red patches showed beneath his white shirt where his nipples used to be. But Micky wasn't aware of it, nor of the broken glass beneath his soles as he opened the back door. He went outside to his dogs and unshackled them. Then they pounced one at a time. A Doberman sank his teeth into Micky's neck but Micky pulled himself free and ran to the fence as they pursued him. He leaped over the fence and kept running, all the way to the open beehive in the next garden. Then the bees swarmed across his skin and the dogs pounced as his neighbour ran towards him. As Micky saw the figure in white approach he thought of the starched white uniform his nanny used to wear and he tasted jam as the dogs sank their teeth into his face and the blood dripped into his mouth and he saw day become night in the blink of an eye. He thought he could see the stars come out. Then he realised he was seeing the cupboard full of knives, their blades sparkling against the wood. The dogs were snarling as they bit him, but to Micky the sound of the swarm was louder. The bees stung him and stung the dogs. Micky thought of the knives and he lost himself in the polished steel of their blades as the insistent sound of a siren rose above the noise of the bees.

77

Karen and Julius were drinking wine at his flat when she got the call from the neighbour. She put the phone down and turned to Julius.

'It's Micky, he's dead.'

'Gary Krane?'

'No, something so weird. He was eaten by his own dogs as bees attacked him, he had this thing about bees, it's a long story.'

'Where did this happen?'

'At his house, my house.'

'Then you have nothing more to fear from him.'

That afternoon they went there together, to the house in Sheen that still felt like Micky's to Karen. She spoke to the police. They took the dogs away and left her and Julius alone together. She wanted him to make love to her there in the kitchen. The idea of doing it in the bedroom made her feel uncomfortable. He stayed the night and they slept in the guest room. And Julius made long slow love to her.

Karen slept deeply, unaware of the moonlight that fell across the sheets. She was also unaware of the sound of footsteps shortly after midnight on the gravel drive, and of the front door being opened, and the alarm deactivated. The intruder climbed the staircase silently. He wore leather gloves as he opened the bedroom door and stared at the empty bed. Then he went into the next room, where Karen and Julius were sleeping.

When Micky called Gary Krane after he left Julius's flat, he told him what had happened and asked for help. He added that if Gary didn't hear back from him that evening to come and get rid of Julius and Karen. Gary had a key and knew the alarm code. Micky had given him the address of Julius's flat. He'd been there and forced the lock, and left after seeing the flat was empty. Now he stood in the spare room and looked down at them as they slept. He'd do the boyfriend first then he'd have a little fun with Karen before he killed her too. Gary pulled the Luger from the back of his belt and moved forwards.

As he did Julius rolled off the bed and caught him with a right hook that knocked Gary to the floor. Then Julius pulled the gun from his hand and emptied the magazine into his head. Gary barely saw his face, this handsome stud killing him. He didn't hear Karen's screams at the sound of gunfire. Afterwards Julius turned on the light. He stared down at Gary, his eyes open, empty now.

'Micky's boyfriend came to finish off what he couldn't do,' he said.

'Julius you've just killed him.'

'What was I meant to do? He was standing over the bed with a gun in his hand.'

'You'll go to prison.'

'Not if they don't find the body.'

'The police will investigate.'

'They'll have to know Gary Krane is missing. How much do you think they'll care if someone has offed him?'

'Tell me what we need to do.'

'I have a place in Norfolk, it's deserted, we can get rid of the body there.'

Julius talked her through it. He emptied Gary's pockets. He cut the carpet away and rolled Gary Krane's body inside it. Karen packed some things, then she backed her car up to the front door and Julius put the body in the boot. Julius went out to the road and saw Gary's car. Then he looked at Gary's recent emails on his phone. There was one Gary had sent a few hours earlier, that read, 'I need a Hundred Percent on this and now I find out he's otherwise engaged.'

Julius drove while Karen followed. He stopped in a deserted road some miles away and left the Bentley there, throwing the keys into some bushes. He got in the Mercedes and Karen drove to his flat where he slung a few things in a case and fixed the lock. Then they left, driving through the night to Norfolk. It was dark as Julius told her to stop the car near a deserted beach. Julius got out and put Gary's mobile in a dustbin. Then he took the body out of the boot. She watched as he walked to the end of a jetty then he disappeared from sight. There was a lengthy pause, and Karen heard the night, the sounds of animals in nearby undergrowth, and of things moving outside the car which she could not identify. She began to feel afraid. She didn't see Julius stoop and cut the plastic, nor did she see him puncture Gary's abdomen with the filleting knife he'd taken from his flat as he released the gases from his abdomen. It was too dark for Karen to see more than a few feet beyond the window and all she saw were the shadows and blurred shapes of plants and the broken coastline. Julius washed the blade of the knife in the water then tied the plastic up with rope. Then he threw Gary in. He walked a few steps further and threw Gary's wallet and the house keys into the water. Julius emerged out of the shadows and put the knife in the boot of Karen's Mercedes before he got back in. He gave her directions to the house.

They arrived as dawn broke pink across the sky. It was an old fishing house, near a canal, somewhat run down but with a charm Karen warmed to. Julius showed her the living room, kitchen, downstairs bathroom, then the two bedrooms upstairs and the bathroom. They went to bed and slept until noon. They spent an idle day and Karen thought of ways to improve the place. The furniture was old, and the carpets frayed, but they were there, and that was all that mattered.

Karen felt elated at the thought of a new life, just him and her and all the sex she wanted. She wanted to explore it all, through the erotic night, his hands wandering across her body like a sexual song, her exulting in the soft melody of his touch, his hard penetrations of her desires, raising her pleasure and taking away the craving she'd felt for too long. And she wondered if she would no longer feel it, the craving, now she had him and Micky was gone.

They went shopping for food and basic provisions at 4:00 PM. They didn't see the car following them.

78

Ashley was driving a hired Ford, her fingers white on the steering wheel. She'd seen them leave Julius's flat and tailed them all the way to Norfolk then lost them at a bend. She'd spent the night driving around trying to find the road where her lover had vanished and she saw them leave a shop. Now as she followed them she thought of all the things she wanted to say to the other woman. She thought of Julius shackled there at her flat. Her anger was arousing her, she would get rid of her rival. She imagined him touching her. She saw secret fingerings in darkened rooms, and women high on him, lost in endless Eros. Her jealousy consumed her as she began to tingle as she thought of Julius's hands on her body. But her desire was scarred, her anger shackled to her need.

Ashley got a puncture as she drove and was forced to stop, watching the Mercedes disappear on another bend. Alone on a stretch of deserted road she thumbed down a passing van. The driver got out and opened her boot and told her she had no spare, and that he'd drive her to the nearest garage.

She got in with him and he drove her away as it began to rain, small hard drops hitting his windshield. She thought of Julius, alone with the other woman. The driver didn't speak to her as he drove, and she looked at him, taking him in. He was a handsome man, and he took her to the deserted car park of a small hotel with a faded sign outside that read, 'Motorway Inn.' Ashley wondered what he was doing there as she stared at the darkened windows and the rain hitting the glass. The driver leaned across the passenger seat. He had something in his hand.

As Ashley tried to open her door and get out she briefly glimpsed what he was holding. Then she stuffed the bra into her mouth.

79

Monday 8:00 AM.

When Karen awoke it was with the knowledge that Micky had been removed from her life and could no longer stand between her and Julius. The sense of relief was quickly displaced by the fear of detection, of a police investigation that would result in her loss of him. And that was too hard to bear. She rose and made coffee and took it into the bedroom. The sun was passing through the curtains and it touched Julius's face as he woke and she kissed him on the mouth.

'Sleep well?' she said.

'Yes, I did as a matter of fact.'

'I've been thinking about the events of the last few days.'

'It's understandable. It will take time.'

'You know it's like I never knew Micky, who was I married to?'

'A homosexual who hated women.'

'I was just there so he could pretend.'

'Some men have to hide who they are.'

He made love to her that morning in which they had no appointments and nowhere to go, no one to avoid or fear. And Karen thought of how long they could stay there. Her mobile rang and Karen saw Tammy's name flash up on the screen and ignored it. Later, as Julius showered, she played the message.

'Karen can you call me,' Tammy said, 'I've found out something about Gary and Micky that you need to know. I think you're in more danger than I realised.'

But Gary and Micky were gone and Karen erased the message. Then she joined her lover in the shower and they went out to eat lunch.

In Fulham, Tammy was discussing her concerns with Arlene. She had her computer screen angled so Arlene could see the file she'd brought up on The Beekeeper.

'There's a link from him straight to Gary Krane,' Tammy said.

'Then it's not just Micky and Gary who Karen needs to be afraid of,' Arlene said.

'No, it's much worse than that.'

'You need to reach her.'

'She's not answering her phone.'

'The Beekeeper had gone quiet, but you think he's a threat to Karen.'

'I think he's active again.'

80

2:00 PM.

Ashley tried to see in the darkness. The day before was a haze, one in which she woke to the strange room and the man who'd abducted her talking about bees. The gag was hurting her mouth. The room smelt dank and there was no sound at all. Then she heard a door opening and saw light through the blindfold. There was a strange smell, like plastic, she thought, then she realised that was not it. She felt a callused hand brush her cheek.

'There precious,' he said.

The voice had a regional accent and she tried to place it as he removed the blindfold and all the months of lovemaking by Julius began to fall away into an old abandoned memory, rotting beneath the surface of her mind. She saw a flash of steel in the darkness and she flinched, and then she remembered the gang rape all those years ago in the back seat of the car where the boys took it in turns with the model who sneered at them. That was the memory she'd turned into the story she told to Julius as he took her on the ride to ecstasy.

'You better promise to behave,' he said, as he began to untie the ropes that tethered her hands to the back of the wooden chair.

Being tied like this made her think of the cuffs she used with Julius. Ashley realised that Julius had given her the thing she'd craved all those years ago, alone with rapists and her teenage dreams. The word seduction hissed at the window pane like an erotic exhalation. As she clawed at their faces she felt only the damp condensation dripping down the panes and their hands on her and fear. Now as this stranger removed her blindfold and gag and she looked into his face he was them again, those boys who took her self-respect one night. And she had taken a subtle form of revenge for years, a latent dominatrix in designer clothes, staring down at men from the tops of her stiletto heels. And now this man who'd abducted her and brought her to this cold room was taking it all away, taking her back to the night she was broken in like a bitch at a stud farm. She wanted Julius to save her. She wanted to believe her lies again as he touched her skin. He had his fingers on her lips and she thought she could taste honey. She looked at him. He was middle aged, with large hands and a heavy build. She imagined him to be a workman as she stood up and rubbed the circulation back into her legs. Then he put on some rubber gloves, working them between his fingers.

'What are you doing?' she said.

'Rubber, I love it, don't you? Condoms, latex, rubber gloves, tyres, inhale it.'

'It's a kinky turn on. Is that what you need from me?'

'You'd do better asking that to The Pimp. He likes whores, I like bees.'

'You put honey on my lips.'

'I want them to kiss you before they sting, pleasure and pain, rubber and bees.'

'What do bees have to do with rubber?'

'Dripping latex and dripping come, just like honey and a woman's sexual fluid.'

'You're in the papers, you're The Beekeeper.'

'I know all about hives, I know all about how to make you right for the honey.'

'Do they turn you on, the bees?'

'Don't they turn you on?'

'I understand about the need to kill, but not in this way, you need the ritual.'

'What do you know about murder or bees?'

'I know about knives and rape, about sexual rivalry and heartache.'

'You're here for the hive, you will be honey.'

'Have you ever desired a woman?'

'The hive is full of bodies.'

'I think you feel more like an insect than a man.'

'You cannot anger me with words.'

'You like sweet things.'

'I will coat your mouth and let then dance there.'

'Tell me about the rubber.'

'I somehow think you are obsessed with secrecy, that you know about the double lives men lead, but I will tell you I once showed a man called Micky what I can do with a hive, he had a thing about bees, he was so scared of them you see, and he dropped one in some latex and bounced it like a rubber ball. His lover stopped me killing him, I needed his services you see, he hired a man called Hundred Percent to remove a certain interfering woman who was trying to snoop into my affairs, on this occasion he was unable to blow her up, she may be bomb proof but she'll get stung just like you and all the others.'

Ashley could see she was distracting him.

'You want me to dance. That's what you said last night.'

'That's right, put on a show and I might even let you go after I've done with you.'

'How to you want me to dance, do you want a sexy dance?'

'Do it as if you are eating nectar from the rim of a sperm filled condom, lap it up like a pussy cat, I'll even let you pick your tyre.'

'What tyre?'

'The one you are going to stand in while I snap your picture.'

'I thought bees ate pollen.'

'I eat the pollen, you eat the nectar, then I turn you into a rubber doll.'

'Is that a sexual thing? You can have me if you want.'

'I have sex with you when you are rubber.'

'Are you so afraid of skin?' Ashley said.

'I prefer the feel of rubber.'

'Because you're disconnected from the body.'

'The body of a bee and the body of a woman.'

'I know a man who knows the body and all its pleasures.'

'I know a man who knows about rubber.'

'What do you do with the gloves?'

'I remove your liquids.'

'There are other ways of doing that.'

'Dance.'

Ashley began moving, she moved the way she knew he wanted, nice and slow, that sleazy look in her eyes she used on the catwalk. Behind him the window looked out onto the car park. She moved forwards, inching towards him. She reached out to touch him. But he stepped back.

'You don't touch me, I touch you,' he said.

'But it's more fun this way.'

She danced some more. Then she did it, surprising herself with the kick, a move she'd leaned a few years ago at a self-defence class. She hit him straight in the groin and he doubled over. Then she picked up the knife he'd put on a table behind him after he cut the ropes and she stabbed him repeatedly until he wasn't moving.

She opened the door and went upstairs into the decaying house. She found her clothes on the floor in the hallway and she got dressed and left, driving his van for miles until she found the road where she'd left her car. She parked his vehicle and got in her own and drove away, slowly on the flat tyre, until she found a garage and got it changed. Then she drove all the way back to London.

81

It was strange for Karen being there with Julius, alone in Norfolk. It was what she wanted, but not there, not in such an isolated spot away from her life. She began to think about the house in Sheen and the remnants of the life she'd led. And she knew that they were criminals now, two lovers who had crossed a line to stay together. What other choice had Micky left them with, she thought. If you are married to a dangerous man, and he is involved with a killer like Gary Krane, love is bought with a moral compromise.

She and Julius were doing the things that a regular couple did. His lovemaking was no less intense or beautiful than it always had been. And still she wondered about him and other women. But there were none there to tempt him and so she relaxed. Tammy had left several messages on her mobile. She called her that evening, and told her what had happened to Micky.

'Karen where are you?' Tammy said.

'It's OK, we're safe.'

'Gary is after you.'

'He won't find us here.'

'There's something else, there is a direct link between Gary and The Beekeeper.'

'You said you were sure it wasn't Micky.'

'It's not, but Gary hired someone on his behalf.'

The line broke up. Karen didn't answer the call back, she didn't want to disclose what had occurred with Gary. Whatever Tammy was saying about Gary and The Beekeeper was no longer relevant because Micky and Gary were dead. Then she realised she was protecting a killer, one who was the greatest lover she had ever known. She felt cold and poured herself some wine. Julius came into the kitchen then. He'd taken a shower and he smelt of summer orchards. He kissed her on the mouth. And she let his taste wash away the wine.

82

Tammy and Arlene were at home talking about The Beekeeper as Karen and Julius went out to eat at the local village.

'There is an erratic pattern here,' Tammy said. 'The Beekeeper killed four women in the early part of the year and then stopped, why?'

'Your theory was that he was afraid he was about to be caught.'

'Yes and it still is. But how deep does the connection between Gary Krane and The Beekeeper go?'

'OK, you hacked Gary's phone and saw an email you think was sent to The Beekeeper.'

Tammy peered at the pad on which she'd written the email.

'This is what he wrote, '"Save the honey for their lips, I've got a Hundred Percent guarantee I can get rid of the interfering bitch for you."'

'OK so he hired Hundred Percent on behalf of The Beekeeper.'

'To get rid of me,' Tammy said.

'Because you were getting too close.'

'Or did he go through with it? We've seen what the Beekeeper can do with explosives.'

'One thing's for sure, Gary Krane knows him and was in contact with him around the time your offices blew up.'

'And then I'm hired by the woman married to Gary's boyfriend to investigate her husband who she thinks is a killer.'

'Do you think he might go after Karen?' Arlene said.

'The Beekeeper?'

'Yes.'

'Right now I don't know what to make of the connections between them all. Karen is convinced she is out of danger because Micky is dead.'

'Well you better unconvince her.'

'I keep trying and she's not picking up.'

'Can you get a reading on Gary Krane's phone?'

83

Tuesday 1:00 PM.

Ashley had made a call to Maurice Calm when she got back to London. She hired him again, this time to find Julius. He came to her flat that afternoon, saying he'd come up with an address for Julius. He slid several pictures of the Norfolk house across the surface of her coffee table.

'He's owned a house in Norfolk for some years,' Maurice said.

'A nice little get away for him.'

'Extremely remote. It will be hard for you to turn up without him noticing.'

'I want him to notice.'

'Like that is it?'

'Like what?'

'Another woman.'

'I suppose you see this all the time.'

His smile was full of condescension and once again Ashley felt like washing. This grubby little man's presence in her hunt for her lover was an odium she had to bear.

'There's a map that will help you how to find it,' Maurice said, handing it to her. 'As you can see, it is not accessible from the main road and situated on a winding path.'

'How much do I owe you?' Ashley said.

'The usual.'

'Thank you for finding him.'

'It's a pleasure to get one up on Julius Gold,' Maurice said.

She paid him and saw him to the door. As she watched Maurice walk away Ashley had an idea. It was a good idea. It would get Julius back. She was going to turn up with all of his things. She would hand them to him as the other woman watched. She closed the door and began to pack.

84

Ashley had put all of his clothes except for a few items into a case. If her plan failed holding some back would make him come and get them. She thought about the other woman. Her jealousy returned and she drank some wine. She already knew what she would say when she got there. The other woman needed to hear it or it wouldn't work. Julius would come after her. She would have him back. She knew the things she wanted to do to him when he did return. From the moment Ashley had fled the Motorway Inn, passing a series of empty rooms, she hadn't thought about the fact that she'd killed a man, nor who he was.

She put the case in the rented Ford and drove to Norfolk. She had the information Maurice Calm had given her on the passenger seat.

She didn't recall placing the kitchen knife on the back seat. It lay there sparkling in the sunlight as she got onto the motorway. Then images of her abduction flashed into her mind like a series of flashes from an intrusive camera. She could taste honey. She remembered dancing and running, but it all seemed vague, as if another woman had gone through it. She pushed it away and thought of Julius, picking up speed, feeling high behind the steering wheel.

She would give him his things and say enough and leave. Then she would wait for him to come to her flat. Then they would go to bed and she would ride it out of him. Ashley knew men, and Julius would come back. Ashley thought of all the extreme sexual acts she wanted to do to Julius.

The road blurred under her spinning wheels and Ashley retreated further into her thoughts. Not far behind her a Mercedes raced along the motorway.

85

8:00 PM.

Tammy had got a location in Norfolk for Gary Krane's phone. She'd spent the weekend hunting for addresses registered to Julius Gold. She'd found the flat in Kew. She'd also found out he owned a house in Norfolk. Tammy and Arlene left London that evening. They were not far behind Ashley as a pink sun set in the sky, dipping behind the fields that lay scattered beyond the road's edge.

'Gary Krane's phone is in Norfolk also, coincidence?' Tammy said.

'Can't be.'

'It doesn't look good Arlene. I hope we're not too late.'

'If Gary Krane has got to them what are you going to do?'

'If he hasn't already killed them you mean?'

'You're going to shoot him with an unregistered weapon.'

Tammy glanced at her in the passenger seat.

'I can't figure out this connection between Gary and Micky, The Beekeeper and Hundred Percent.'

'Gary hires Hundred Percent to carry out hits, but how well does he know The Beekeeper?'

'What if they're all working together?'

'It would explain how The Pimp has managed to evade detection for so long.'

'You mean we've been spied on by more than one killer?'

'If you think about it it's improbable he could get in and out of our house so easily.'

'But who's running things? I think The Pimp would want to be in charge.'

'So would Gary Krane.'

'OK so Krane hires Hundred Percent, he's a hit man taking on jobs.'

'But he also hires him for a serial killer.'

'Maybe The Beekeeper went to Krane as himself.'

'You mean Krane has no knowledge of what his client is doing as a serial killer?'

'Maybe. Or he may not care.'

'The connection here is that all these men hate women,' Tammy said.

'Right.'

'The Pimp and The Beekeeper have an obsession with lips, they prey on women, Gary Krane is a violent homosexual who hurts young men but probably has hurt women.'

'He'd enjoy what The Pimp and The Beekeeper do.'

'And his boyfriend Micky hates women, think of what Karen has told me about him.'

'There's another explanation, The Pimp and The Beekeeper are the same man.'

'And Gary Krane knows all about him.'

86

Ashley got there before them, stepped straight out of the car with the case, set it down in front of the door and rang the bell. She could see her reflection in the paint, one side of her face illuminated by the sensor light, the other side in shadow, as if she was two people without Julius.

It was Julius who answered and Ashley could see he was angry. She was about to reach out and touch him when instead she handed him the case.

'What's this?' Julius said.

'Your things.'

'You travelled a long way just to give me that. I suspect there's something else behind your visit.'

'You just disappeared, what was I meant to think?'

'It's complicated.'

'Try me.'

'Not now.'

'When then?'

'I'll call you later.'

'Is she in the house?'

'Who?'

'You know who I mean.'

'I don't.'

'The woman I saw you with.'

'Do you mean me?' Karen said.

Julius hadn't seen her come downstairs and along the hallway. Ashley only glimpsed her as she was speaking, her eyes focused on Julius who was standing in the doorway. Now Ashley looked at her, thinking not bad, but she hasn't got what I've got, this should be easy. Karen came right up behind Julius. She and Ashley exchanged the intense jealous glares of sexual rivals.

'Yes I mean you,' Ashley said.

'Are you one of his exes?'

'I am. But not so ex, current.'

'Julius?' Karen said, turning to him.

She'd just had a shower and her hair was wet and she smelled of roses. She'd put on a blue blouse and a black skirt and she looked sexual and predatory.

'Karen this is Ashley,' Julius said.

'You've been seeing her.'

'Yes for a while. She's brought me my things.'

'So it's over between you two?'

Ashley brushed past Julius and Karen and went into the kitchen. They followed her and stood in awkward silence for a few moments, waiting for her to speak. Julius had made fresh coffee and he poured a cup, setting it down on the table. Ashley glanced at it then walked up to Julius.

'I haven't come here for coffee,' she said.

'What have you come here for?' Karen said.

'To take back what's mine.'

'Julius, yours?'

'He's living with me, didn't he tell you?'

'Ashley, you can't come here making demands,' Julius said.

'You owe me an explanation.'

'And I'll give it to you.'

'Give it to me now.' She turned to Karen. 'Are you happy with the fact that he's been seeing both of us?'

'What he did until recently doesn't concern me.'

'It was only the other day. How many other women are there Julius?'

'I think you should leave,' Karen said.

'I want an explanation. I'm the only woman who can satisfy a man like him in bed, do you use cuffs on him, do you use chains?'

'Get out of here. Or I'll press charges for the time you attacked me in the street.'

'Call me,' Ashley said to Julius.

Then she was gone, walking out of the house. Karen and Julius listened to her footsteps fade on the path outside.

87

9:15 PM.

'So you were seeing her,' Karen said.

'For a while but she's obsessive.'

'I was a married woman. I can't expect you not to have seen other women.'

'She had me followed.'

'That time outside your flat?'

'It would appear so.'

'You told me it was to do with debt.'

'The private investigator lied to me.'

'So she's known for some time, why wait until now?'

'I think she hoped to keep me.'

'Were you living with her?'

'I was staying with her.'

'I can't blame her for being obsessed.'

'I think that's the last we'll see of her.'

'I'm not so sure.'

'What makes you say that?'

'Woman's intuition. She wants you back and I think she's determined.'

'I'll call her and tell her it's off.'

'I don't think it's going to be that easy.'
'I wonder how she found me here.'
'How did you meet her?'
'I picked her up.'
'How long were you seeing her?'
'A few weeks, that's all. She'll meet other men.'
'Not like you Julius.'

88

As Ashley got into her car she saw a black Mercedes crunch the gravel drive. She watched Tammy and Arlene get out. Her obsession told her these were more women come to claim Julius. And so she waited to see what happened, hoping that two visits from rivals would see Karen off. She didn't see a white van pull up at the edge of the property, idle and then move slowly forward.

After a long pause Karen answered the door. Julius was coming along the hallway behind her.

'Karen can we come in?' Tammy said.

'Since you've come all this way.'

Karen stepped to one side and led them into the living room, Julius following.

'Tammy this is Julius,' Karen said.

'Are you both OK?'

'Yes, there really is nothing to worry about.'

'Your visit is a surprise,' Julius said.

'I was working for Karen, as you may know. I think she is in danger.'

'She did mention it, you working for her.'

'I think Gary Krane intends to harm you both.'

'I don't think he will,' Julius said.

'How can you be so sure?'

'How will he find us here?'

'I did.'

'If he comes I'll take care of it.'

'You're going to take him on?'

'If I have to. I think you can go back to London.'

'It's more complicated than you think,' Tammy said. 'Gary Krane uses a hit man called Hundred Percent to carry out hits. I think The Beekeeper contacted Gary to have me taken out. My offices were blown up, I was out, but I think it may have been Hundred Percent who did it. I think there is more than one man you need to be afraid of Karen, come back with us.'

'There's really no need,' Karen said.

Just then the sound of Julius's mobile ringing disturbed the conversation.

'I have to take a call,' he said, glancing at caller ID.

But he let it go to his voicemail.

'Tammy it's OK, you can leave us, I'll call if anything happens,' Karen said.

'If that's what you want.'

Karen showed them to the door as Julius went upstairs with his phone.

'I didn't catch your boyfriend's second name,' Tammy said.

'It's Gold.'

Tammy nodded. Karen watched as they walked to their car, then she closed the door and stared at the case that Ashley had left, wanting to go through Julius's things, as if to search for clues about him. And she wondered whether it was simple curiosity about his life with her. She didn't hear the conversation between Tammy and Arlene on the drive.

'He's Holly's lover, my client is having an affair with Julius Gold,' Tammy said.

'And what was it she discovered he was hiding?'

Inside the house Julius was making a call upstairs.

'It's me, Hundred Percent, I can't take on any jobs at the moment,' he said.

89

As Tammy and Arlene got in their car The Pimp reached over the back seat and placed the muzzle of a Colt 45 on the back of Tammy's head.

'You didn't see me lying on the floor, too preoccupied with lover boy in there I suppose,' The Pimp said.

Arlene gasped as she turned round.

'Getting turned on now? You'll gasp for me on film, Arlene. Now Tammy we're going to take a little drive, all four of us, but it's not you who'll be doing the driving, one false move and I blow her brains onto her dashboard, and while that would make a nice effect I imagine, I have other plans for you. You're about to join my collection of lips.'

The Pimp place a piece of chloroformed cloth over Tammy's mouth. He held her firmly against the seat as he angled the gun at Arlene. Then he put her to sleep too. He lugged their bodies to his van and placed them inside it next to Ashley, who lay bound hand and foot on the floor, then he drove away.

His movements went unnoticed from the house. When Julius came back downstairs Karen was pouring herself a glass of Pinot Grigio.

'Do you think they suspect?' she said.

'That I killed Gary Krane?'

'You sounded too sure. I don't know if Tammy bought it.'

'They can't know anything.'

'I'm sure you're right.'

'It's only us who know, Karen.'

'Well they've gone now.'

'Their car's still on the drive.'

90

10:15 PM.

As Julius glanced out of the widow at the Mercedes and the hired Ford, Tammy and Arlene were struggling with the ropes. The Pimp was on the motorway now, sticking to the speed limit. But every time he took a bend the three women were knocked against one another and the sides of the van. Ashley was also trying to get her hands free but he had tied the knots too tight.

As he drove he heard the sound of duct tape being ripped from swollen mouths. He saw lips in drawers, on ice. The landscape sped past his window as he took them there, to his place of cameras and final acts, of deeds he needed to perform to allay the other man he spoke of at times. He'd mentioned him to Tammy.

As he drove, Julius and Karen walked out of the house. Julius opened the doors of the Mercedes then the Ford.

'The keys are still in the engine,' he said.

'Where are they?'

'I'll check the footmarks on the drive.'

'They can't have just gone off for a walk together.'

He saw that none of the footmarks led away from the property. He followed one set of to the van's tyre tracks.

'I think they've been abducted,' he said.

'Who by?'

'Who would want Tammy out of the way?'

'The Pimp.'

91

11:00 PM.

The Pimp drove, thinking of all the things he would do to his whores. He'd gained an extra one, she could be part of the film. He arrived at a house in the Surrey countryside in the early hours of the morning and entered a garage. He got out and closed the door, then he opened the back of the van. The women were lying on their sides staring at him.

'Tammy, Arlene, welcome to my cinema, you're on film already, but there are more scenes to shoot,' he said.

He opened a door on the far side of the garage, lifted Tammy out of the van, hoisting her over his shoulder. Then he carried her up some stone steps to another door which he opened, taking her into a bare windowless room. He deposited her on the floor, closed the door behind him, then got Arlene and Ashley. He removed the duct tape from Ashley's mouth.

'Your driving licence states you're Ashley,' The Pimp said.

'Let me out of here.'

'Do you like cameras? You look like you do.'

'What is this place?'

'A cinema.'

'I need to use the bathroom.'

'All in good time, first you need to perform for me.'

'My boyfriend will have seen you abduct me.'

The Pimp didn't answer her. He untied her, tore the duct tape from Tammy's mouth and undid her ropes, then he did the same for Arlene, his gun trained on them. He watched as the women got to their feet. Then he opened a drawer in a table at the end of the room and removed a camera.

92

The Pimp entered the room carrying a tray with some toast and coffee on it. He laid it on the floor and stared at the women. He'd let Ashley use the bathroom, tethered them to hooks in the stone wall and taken some shots of them then gone to bed. Now he unshackled them one at a time and allowed them to eat. Tammy looked at him, thinking of Joyce's description. He was, as she had said, not bad looking. But he was too remote, like a statute. She thought that his life of watching had engendered a dislocation in him that made it appear as if he was on a screen. He was caught in his own camera lens. He seemed to be watching an inner film. His gaze was directed at Ashley, and his expressionless eyes looked colourless. His grey hair gave him a patrician look that was at odds with who she knew him to be. It softened his face.

Seeing Ashley put the toast in her mouth reminded him of being a boy, brought up by a mute mother whose silence unnerved him. It reminded him of being forced to eat food he abhorred by his vicious nanny who would gag him if he disobeyed her. Now he had mouths before him, mouths he could use. He thought of the film, he thought of new images he could introduce into it. He watched the women eat, like animals in his zoo. This was the place where he'd killed Holly, and many women before her. Now he had Tammy and her lover and this other woman. He'd start with her.

'I'm going to play you a film then you can go on camera,' he said when they had finished.

He opened the door at the far end of the room and watched as they went into a room whose walls were covered in plasma screens.

'This is the cinema,' The Pimp said.

Then he flicked a remote control and flooded the room with images of Tammy and Arlene making love. But the images had been doctored and cut to show them doing things they had never done. In one shot neither of them had a mouth. The women looked away, past him at the room they'd come from and the door back to the garage.

'You won't be leaving here with lips,' he said.

Then he turned the lights off.

93

He left them there alone with the film, he left them for the morning while he prepared his tools. The Pimp had made many tools over the years, he had a collection of knives of differing lengths with handles shaped to fit his hand. But what he particularly enjoyed using were what he called his body part tools, cutting implements shaped like female tongues and breasts. He picked up a knife in the shape of a tongue. The blade was razor sharp. On a work bench lay breast knives with nipples, as sharp as needles. He had skewers he liked to drive through tongues when he sent them in the post. He had an array of implements which could cut the flesh in varying ways. He'd made many tools over the years. And now he considered which weapon he would use on each of the women. He enjoyed this stage of things, the preparation for the editor's cut.

He returned to the cinema and put the lights on and stopped the film. The women blinked, their eyes adjusting to the light.

'Ashley you can perform for us,' The Pimp said, 'then it's you, Tammy and Arlene, I'll even give you the rest of Holly for you troubles.'

'What is all this about performing?' Ashley said.

'He films women, without their knowing,' Tammy said.

'I guess you know they refer to me as The Pimp, that I'm labelled a serial killer.'

'You are a serial killer.'

'Tammy, your sister said a few things before I cut her up. She told me all about your little hang ups.'

'You know you can try to distort her all you want but you can't remove my memory of her.'

'You know she loved it when I touched her.'

'You're deluded, and insane.'

'Oh yes, I'm a serial killer,' he said and brushed her lips with his fingers.

Tammy backed against the wall.

'Why do you collect lips?' she said.

'Beneath the utterance lies the sin, beyond the lips lies the tongue.'

'I hear you have a tattoo.'

'That bitch Joyce been talking again?'

'You have the word "Lies" on your chest, isn't that right?'

'Want to take a peek?'

'What are the lies?'

'I'm looking at one of them.'

'You think women are liars and whores.'

'Can you prove me wrong?'

'Where do you get your sexual kicks? Is it in the watching or the cutting?'

'I'd say a little of both.'

'And then there's the prostitutes.'

'I like a little equality in the work force don't you?'

'You don't know the meaning of the word.'

'You might think you're a private dick but you still trade in flesh Tammy.'

'Why didn't you leave my gun at the scene when you shot Joyce?'

'Because that would have got you put away and I'd miss out on the whoring you're about to offer me.'

'The missing piece of Holly's letters, what was it she discovered about Julius Gold?'

'He's an interesting fella, I can tell you.'

'You have the rest of the letters here don't you?'

'I have a lot of her here.'

'Why don't you show us?'

'Playing for time Tammy?'

'It's sexual isn't it?'

'What's sexual?'

'Your problem, your need to watch.'

'And I thought you wanted to know about Julius Gold. You're curious how he got her turned on, dike and all, just like you, maybe you'd like to give him a try.'

'What did she find out about him?'

'That he was a killer in bed.'

'Do you know him?'

'Only through Holly's porn.'

'She said he was a great lover. He's a contrast to you, The Pimp, able only to abduct and torture.'

'Do you know why I am called The Pimp? Because I find all the whores.'

'You know, if I had my Glock in my hand I'd shoot you right now.'

'I bet you love holding it, like holding a dick in your fist, right?'

'You took shots of me visiting Joyce and pinned them to her breasts.'

'I did more than that, I raped her with your weapon Tammy, stuffed it down her lying throat and broke two of her teeth before I abducted the man the police were looking for. I brought him here for a lesson in tool making. I bet you want to know all about it, how I did it. No one saw me coming or going because the next door neighbour got a call about the Inland Revenue, a friend of mine made it for me, provided a little distraction for the street snooper.'

'What friend?'

'A man called Marcus Needle. You may know him as The Beekeeper.'

'You're saying you know The Beekeeper?'

'We used to belong to the midnight club.'

'What's that?'

'The midnight club was set up by Gary Krane, that's right. He used to get young men and women round and cut them. Marcus used to go, so did I, before we got our careers going. Sadism is such a suburban kick I find. It gets tedious after a while. The groans you see are so predictable, they sound like porn, whereas you and Arlene make it all so real.'

'You know Gary Krane.'

'Come on Tammy you must have guessed there was a connection somewhere.'

'You got The Beekeeper to call Joyce's neighbour.'

'We talk from time to time. You could say I have a certain influence over him, gave him sound career advice, how to work out all his problems with the sweet stuff.'

'Why are you telling me this? You've given away his identity.'

'The Beekeeper got stung, he's going nowhere. I went round to buy some honey and found him chopped up. He has a hotel you see, someone got to him, I left one of your kitchen knives there, he no longer needs to be protected against the law, but you do, snooping Tammy, The Pimp's whore, the dike with a penchant for guns she can't use.'

As he was speaking Ashley watched him intently.

'Do you still talk to Gary Krane?' Tammy said.

'No, you see he had this boyfriend called Micky who is scared of bees and did something Marcus didn't like. It nearly ended with murder, Gary talked Marcus out of it and that was around the time we left them to it, the two poofs. I told Marcus what he needed to do, gave him the idea for all the rubber and the honey. He was obsessed with penetration by sharp objects, hung up on needles and stings, he liked bees, it seemed a natural progression.'

'You, The Beekeeper, Gary Krane and Micky.'

'It seems unlikely doesn't it? Then again look at most college reunions, what little do they have in common apart from a zest for ostentation? At least we enjoyed our parties. The Beekeeper was troubled, he needed to release his sexual angst, and I gave him a few ideas, it's easy with a man who enjoys honey. He does me favours from time to time.'

'How long ago was this?'

'A few years ago. I bet you'd have liked to go along, be part of it all.'

'You and a bunch of sick men cutting people.'

'You see, I told you you'd get aroused.'

'I'm not aroused, I'm sick, sick to the gut at you.'

The Pimp turned and looked at Ashley. And as she stared into his translucent eyes she saw only herself, as if he had become a mirror for the women he preyed on. His eyes looked as hard as glass and Ashley saw herself there like an insect trapped in amber, her face frozen by the moment and her fear.

He grabbed Arlene with one hand, as she tried to pull away, but he held her tight.

'Ready for a little action?' he said to Tammy.

'What do you want us to do?'

'I want you to do what you did on film. I want you to be the main bitch in this drama.'

The Pimp threw Arlene at her then he pulled a knife from the leather sheath at the back of his belt.

'Tammy where's your tongue?' he said.

He jabbed Arlene with the knife, cutting her arm and drawing blood. He pointed at the floor, and Tammy and Arlene lay down. Tammy did it the way he wanted it, kissing Arlene on the cold floor. The Pimp stood over them watching, his arms folded across his chest. Tammy tried to think of ways of getting away, of weapons she could use on him, but they were trapped. She wanted to shoot him through the heart.

94

After the performance The Pimp left them in the room with the bare walls. The women talked of ways of getting away, of how to attack him together, but they knew any attempt might end in him killing them. Then The Pimp returned with a chair which he set in the middle of the room. He laid a tongue knife down on a table next to it. He walked over to Arlene and grabbed her arm.

'Sit down,' he said.

As she walked towards the chair she grabbed the knife and cut his arm as Tammy lunged at him. He punched Tammy, knocking her to the floor and got the knife off Arlene.

'Tie her up Tammy,' he said, opening a drawer in the table and tossing a rope at her.

'Is this where you kill us?' she said.

'Oh no, not yet. Do it or I'll cut her throat.'

'I recognise this room.'

'It's where I cut off Holy's lips.'

Tammy tied Arlene to the chair.

'You said something to me on the phone once,' she said.

'I said many things to you on the phone while I watched your every move.'

'You mentioned you were performing a service for someone at your house, getting him his whores and taking their lips away.'

'That's right, that's why I am not a serial killer.'

'So who is he and who is The Pimp?'

95

He left them in the room, he left them for what seemed like a long time and Tammy wondered now if it was the work of two men. She'd read about collaborations between killers before, they were rare but not unheard of. She tried to fathom what relationship The Pimp would have with The Beekeeper. From what she knew about him he would have to be in charge. The idea that he was procuring women for someone else did not match his profile. Or was The Beekeeper waiting to turn them into rubber in the next room?

Then he came in. They stared at a man in a mask with a huge pair of lips on it. He was wearing a leather apron and leather gloves. He had a steel girder in his hands.

'I am the brothel keeper,' he said.

'Your voice, it's the same. Is this how you dress up when you kill?' Tammy said.

'What do you think this is for? Does The Pimp work with steel?'

'You're a toolmaker, aren't you?'

She looked at the sharpened ends of the girder.

'My tools are your flesh, your bodies are mine, you yield. I made you what you are, stars for a day or more on my sex film, welcome to the place where Holly lost her tongue, but if you think The Pimp is the one who knows all about lips then you are wrong, he brings them to me, they are mine. Open your mouth Tammy, I have something sweet for your palate.'

'Is this the only way you can have sex?'

'Do you think the metal is about sex?'

'He will fuck you before you die, that is what you told me.'

'I use the steel to penetrate, you like it that way.'

'You are The Pimp, aren't you?'

'I am what you see before you. Do I dress like The Pimp?'

'I think you're split, I think the way you have survived is to be two men in one body.'

'For all your theories you're still just a whore.'

'Do you think they won't catch you? Even if you kill us all now.'

'Did you catch me Tammy? For all your spying you never knew when I came and went.'

'It's you who's the spy.'

'I'm going to make you wear the thong after I kill Arlene.'

'If you kill her I'll put a bullet in your head.'

'That would be a neat trick. How are you going to do that?'

'I'll find a way.'

'Do you know what happens now Tammy?'

'Show us your face.'

But he didn't, he simply swung the girder back. And Tammy raced to push Arlene's chair out of the way.

11:30 AM.

Tammy managed to get to her just in time and she and Arlene ended up on the floor. Then the door from the garage swung open and Julius came in with Tammy's Glock. Tammy heard the shots, as Julius fired twice, and The Pimp fell to the ground. Julius stood over him and removed the mask and stared into the blank eyes of the man who had collected lips, then he emptied the gun into his head. The room was full of smoke and the smell of cordite. Tammy walked over to the body of the man she'd hunted for months.

'So who was The Pimp?' she said.

'Maybe we'll never know,' Julius said.

'I don't want to leave without looking. There must be some evidence in this house.'

'You're looking for an explanation for what motivated him to do the things he did.'

Tammy nodded, then they went through the building. It was a small house that had no sense of being a home. They looked, Tammy and Julius leading the way, Arlene and Ashley following, looking on. They found rooms full of body parts and knives, of tools and boxes of DVD's that Tammy assumed contained films of the women The Pimp spied on. The kitchen was bare, containing only some tinned food and a dustbin full of take away food. It spoke of the lifestyle of a man with no ties to anything except the homicidal vigilance he exerted over women. The single bedroom housed only a bed and chair. And one thing that was remarkable was that there were no pictures on the walls, apart from in one room dedicated to the images he'd taken of his victims. That was decorated with countless shots of women naked, with the tip of a knife pressed to their skins. There was a tool making room, containing various tools and a lathe. One room contained a filing cabinet and Tammy went through it methodically, seeking a name for the man who killed Holly. There were cuttings from the newspapers about his crimes, the usual vanity of a killer, and articles about lips. The Pimp had studied the anatomy of the mouth, he was particularly interested in the elasticity of lips. Tammy went through it all, from the clippings to the images of women. She found his toolmaker's certificate. Then she found his driving licence, studying it closely. The picture matched his face, and gave him to be forty-two years old with no endorsements. The address was in Surrey and she assumed it was registered to the building where he took his victims.

'The Pimp was Bernard Mack,' she said, showing it to Julius.

'A mack is a pimp, there's the connection,' Julius said.

'There was the clue in the name he used. Still, it doesn't tell me what motivated him to do what he did to women.'

'I remember reading about him. There was an article in the papers years ago about what makes someone into a killer,' Julius said.

'You mean Bernard Mack was wanted as a killer?'

'No. The article looked at conditioning and DNA. It mentioned two cases of boys who'd been abused and how they turned out. Gerald Yard was one of the boys.'

'He's believed wrongly by the police to have been responsible for the killings that were the work of The Pimp,' Tammy said.

'Gerald Yard had a mother who used to force him to eat offal as a punishment, to eat it naked. He ended up collecting the body parts of his female victims. The article then discussed the case of Bernard Mack. He was taken into care as a teenager when social services found cuts on his body. He had a mute mother and a nanny who routinely abused him. She scarred him with kitchen knives. The conclusion was that he'd been allowed to lead a normal life by being placed in a good home, rehabilitated from the abuse in such a way that any attendant danger resulting from what he'd been through had been nullified. The article was trying to peddle the idea that social services can rescue kids from the fate of Gerald Yard, who became a killer.'

'It seems it was a piece of social propaganda that mentioned a man who turned out just the opposite of the way it described him,' Tammy said.

'And the irony is, it was in the home he was sent to where he first watched tool making. The foster father was a tool maker.'

'And Bernard Mack ended up making his own brand of knives. It was as if, returned to normality, he saw everything through jaded eyes.'

'I saw the knife shaped like a tongue. His obsessions were his way of addressing what had been done to him, of offsetting how scarred he felt.'

'Bernard Mack watching tools being made, thinking of his own uses for them. If I'd read that article I would have known who had killed Holly.'

Julius took them out of there, down the stairs and past the van and out into the fresh air. Arlene kissed Julius on the mouth. They got into Karen's Mercedes. Then he drove them away. He stopped at a garage and bought them water and sandwiches and waited as they ate them, noticing Tammy's eyes on him in the rear view mirror.

'How did you know he'd taken us?' Tammy said.

'I saw your cars on the drive. There were foot marks leading to another set of tyre tracks, and I found you through the GPS on Ashley's phone.'

'Where's Karen?'

'At the house in Norfolk.'

'No sign of Gary?'

'No.'

'It doesn't add up that he would disappear like that.'

Julius said nothing as he took them back to London. He dropped Ashley off at her flat first.

'Are you coming back?' she said.

'Not today.'

'Call me.'

'I will.'

Then he took Tammy and Arlene to Fulham.

'You're going back to Norfolk?' Tammy said as she was getting out.

'Yes.'

'Do you want a coffee before you do?'

'That would be good.'

As he sat in her living room she said it. It had been on her mind all the way there.

'You're Hundred Percent aren't you?'

'I'm not sure I follow you.'

'You're the hit man Gary Krane used to carry out a series of hits on rival businessmen.'

'I think you're in shock.'

Julius stood up but Tammy caught it, that moment of recognition in his eyes. She also knew he could never admit to it.

'I think he may even have considered hiring you to blow up my offices. I don't think he did, I think The Beekeeper did it, he liked using explosives. You saved our lives, so anything you may have done in the line of work I am going to ignore. There's something I would like you to have before you leave.
'

She left him there for a few minutes and returned with Holly's letters.

'You knew my sister,' she said, handing them to him.

Julius glanced at the cover then looked at Tammy and she saw it in his eyes, the two men, the lover who gave women endless pleasure and the killer.

'At least you have the satisfaction of knowing her killer is dead,' he said.

'The way you took The Pimp out, it was a professional job.'

'I better go back to Karen.'

'Did you know The Beekeeper?'

'Only what I read in the papers.'

'Ashley said something to me while we were held by The Pimp, she mentioned being abducted by a man obsessed by rubber.'

Julius handed Tammy her Glock.

'I found that in your car, it's a good gun.'

'And I bet you know all about weapons.'

'I know a bit about them.'

'Holly found out, didn't she? About your other life.'

She watched him walk to the Mercedes, start it up and leave the street. Arlene was sitting on the sofa, a glass of Pinot Grigio in her hand when she went back in.

'Are you just going to leave it like that?' she said.

'He saved our lives.'

'He's a hit man.'

'He's a hit man and he worked for Gary Krane. He's not a killer in the way The Pimp or The Beekeeper are, I don't track hit men.'

'You really think it's him?'

'Yes, I think he's Hundred Percent.'

'What about his other life?'

'There are two of him, the lover who gives women endless pleasures, and the killer. He's a gigolo I guess, and I'd say Julius Gold is addicted to dangerous situations.'

'And pleasure.'

'The danger of sex, with other men's wives, and killing, they're both highs.'

'When he's not carrying out hits he's seducing women?'

'That pretty much sums it up,' Tammy said.

'You wonder what he'd be like?'

'It crossed my mind.'

'The Pimp was split, dislocated from the past and whatever had driven him to kill.'

'Yes, Julius is not, he inhabits two worlds, and that's part of his appeal.'

'And they're both killers.'

'Of a different kind. Julius is himself when he fires a gun.'

'And when he fucks.'

'Yes he's a killer in bed, women get hooked on him, Holly did.'

'Do you think he'd ever harm Karen?'

'No I don't, I think he's firmly the lover with women, he kills for money.'

'And what do you think has happened to Gary Krane?'

'I think Julius has killed him, that's why he and Karen have been so confident about saying they don't think they will be troubled by him.'

'What about The Beekeeper, what do you think has happened to him?'

'That I don't know.'

Tammy poured herself a glass of wine, took a sip and topped Arlene up.

'What now?' Arlene said.

'The Pimp's gone, we have the house all to ourselves.'

97

Tammy had called Karen and got Ashley's number off Julius, wanting to speak to her. She'd left a message for her and that morning Ashley called her back.

'Ashley, while we were held by The Pimp you mentioned being abducted by a man,' Tammy said.

'Yes, I think I blanked it out but it's come back to me out of a haze.'

'Can you tell me what happened? I think the man who abducted you was the killer known as The Beekeeper.'

'It was a few days before The Pimp took us. I'd broken down and a man gave me a lift. He said he'd take me to a garage. He took me to a hotel. When I came to I was tied up. He coated my mouth with honey, he had this thing with rubber. He wore rubber gloves and wanted me to dance.'

'How did you get away?'

'I stabbed him and ran, I think I killed him.'

'You killed the serial killer known as The Beekeeper.'

'Another killer?'

'For a while I thought he and The Pimp were the same person, now I know they weren't.'

'I keep going over and over it in my mind asking myself should I tell the police.'

'No, there's no point, when it comes to this kind of crime they're inept, you'd be tried. You have nothing to reprimand yourself with.'

Ashley gave her a description of where The Beekeeper had taken her. She and Arlene drove there that day. They found the hotel but it had been burned to the ground, only the sign gave away that they were in the right place. They stared at the blackened windows and the crumbling façade. Behind the building were two hives, the only sign of life. Bees flew out and darted into the few flowers in the derelict garden.

'Another one of The Pimp's games?' Tammy said.

'Maybe he came to destroy the evidence.'

And so they drove away from the building where The Beekeeper had turned women into rubber dolls, where he had used his honey. Tammy made a call to Ashley on the way.

'We found it but it's burnt down,' she said.

'It wasn't like that when I left it.'

'I think The Pimp came here. I think he found The Beekeeper's body and set fire to the place.'

'If I hadn't escaped I know what he would have done to me.'

'Ashley think of this, you've got away from two killers.'

'Yes, that's cause for celebration.'

'Do something to celebrate.'

'I know what I want to do.'

Tammy ended the call and she and Arlene returned to the office. She sorted through some paperwork and thought about whether she wanted to continue with the business.

'You know, now that Holly's killer is dead I don't know if I want to spend my days tracking killers,' she said.

'Someone has to catch them,' Arlene said.

'Yes, and it's not going to be the police. You know I keep thinking about why The Beekeeper killed Marjorie Tram.'

'It's another way of saying he knew about you, just like The Pimp.'

Tammy noticed an envelope in her in tray. She recognised the style in which it was addressed and knew who it was from before she opened it. 'Melt the wax doctor for all that honey,' was typed across the front. Tammy opened it and read the content of the final message from The Pimp.

'Hey whore,

I bet you wonder how Dr Tram got turned into a rubber doll. The Beekeeper told me all about it, how he was one of her patients and she had this thing for dick. Like you. I bet you wanted to get her in the sack. He set her up, he's good at that. He took her to his hotel and put the wick in her head. It was him who cancelled the appointment the day you gashed your feet. He got you to see the doctor as I went to your house. I dig your taste in lingerie but I know what I want you to wear. Then again, did you know Dr Tram was an abortionist? No shit. She liked to dig out the babies from her clients' wombs. I got a little annoyed when the Beekeeper told me he tried to blow you up. I want you all to myself, and now I am going to have you, gash and all, you and that cutie

Arlene. After all, what use is charred meat? I like mine pink and raw. You're going to love the film of Holly dancing. The blood running down her thighs. I've left another piece of her for you, see if you can find it.

Yours in surveillance and procurement,

The Pimp.'

'So The Beekeeper killed Marjorie because she was my doctor,' Tammy said. 'He and The Pimp were working closely together.'

'And then there's the midnight club, a bunch of sick men who got together to indulge in sadism, it's like a breeding ground for killers,' Arlene said.

'It ties them all together, The Pimp, The Beekeeper, Gary and Micky. But Micky was the weak one, dominated by Gary and afraid of his own sexuality.'

'And they're all dead.'

Tammy opened the top drawer of her desk and screamed. There lying on white tissue paper was a foetus. She knew it was Holly's. Arlene looked in the drawer and began to weep.

'How many more things has he left?' she said.

'That's it, there's nothing more he can deposit here or at the house,' Tammy said.

'What do we do with it? Should you find out if it is Holly's?

'No need, it has to be, I'll deal with it in the morning.'

She wrapped her arms around Arlene and consoled her. Then they left the office to return home, aware for once they were not being watched.

As they did Ashley was calling Julius. She knew when she spoke to Tammy how she wanted to celebrate her escape from two killers.

'Are you coming back to live with me?' she said.

'It's complicated.'

'You want Karen or me?'

'I want both of you.'

'Julius come to me and put your hands on me. What if The Pimp had killed us?'

'I'll come when I can Ashley.'

'What is it, that thing you keep hidden?'

'There are some letters I might show you, they'll make sense of it for you.'

98

8:00 PM.

Karen was standing by the sofa in the living room in Norfolk as Julius got off the phone.

'You don't have to make a choice,' Karen said.

'You're talking about what I said to Ashley?'

'I heard. After all, I know what it's like to be a prisoner.'

'Let's go back to Sheen.'

He touched her, he took her upstairs and kissed her in the bedroom before they left. Then he drove her back to London.

They sat in the kitchen and drank coffee as Julius got Holly's letters and laid them in front of Karen. And she read them.

'Another woman obsessed by you, she was Tammy's sister,' Karen said when she got to the last one.

'I went out with her for a while.'

'But what's the connection? I remember how you reacted when I told you I'd hired Tammy, you didn't like it.'

'She tracks killers Karen.'

'Yes.'

'There is something missing in the letters.'

'What it was she found out about you.'

'Yes.'

'What is it, what are you hiding?'

'I'm a contract killer, I was worried she was onto me.'

For a moment Micky's face flashed before Karen's eyes, she could see him standing in the kitchen with a jar of jam, his fists clenched above his belt.

'You're not like them, The Pimp, you're not even like Micky,' Karen said.

'No, and I'm picky about the jobs I take on.'

'But there's something else isn't there?'

'I knew Gary Krane, I didn't know your husband.'

'The way you killed them, the way you got rid of the bodies, it all makes sense.'

'I want you to know. I'm also giving the work up.'

'I think I'm attracted to dangerous men, Julius.'

'When I met you in Attic, it was just you and me.'

'And it still is, you've kept Attic alive all these weeks.'

He took them to Ashley that night. He stood outside her door beneath a burning blue sky sprinkled with silver stars and he entered her hallway with the letters.

'These answer your question,' he said.

'About the other you.'

He nodded and she went into the living room. She sat on the sofa with her legs tucked under her and read them.

'What was it she discovered?' Ashley said, closing the letters.

'I'm a hit man.'

'It makes sense. It all makes sense.'

'Don't you see, sex is about danger?'

'You're a killer in bed, but you're a killer.'

'So what do you want to do?'

'You're not like the men who abducted me.'

'The obsession you had that I was hiding something was because of that.'

'You lead two lives. I want both of you to fuck me, the lover and the killer.'

'How different do you think it would be?'

'I'm addicted to you.'

'What about other women?'

'What about them Julius?'

She draped her arms around his neck and kissed him on the mouth.

'Make love to me,' she said.

He did, on the sofa without cuffs or chains. And Ashley fell into him, all of him, the whole of Julius whom she'd hungered for in all the weeks of craving.

'I understand why I got so hooked on you, it's because of the danger just below the surface of your skin.'

'I picked up Kitten Rogers in a bar, I bedded Ashley Greene.'

'And you can bed me some more, you can come here any time.'

'I'll visit you in the small hours, and enter your fantasies.'

'You saved my life my beautiful killer.'

He left and returned to Sheen. Karen was waiting for him in bed in the spare bedroom. She didn't ask him how it went with Ashley. She knew.

'She'll go on wanting you,' she said as Julius got undressed.

'It seems that way.'

'No place for jealousy in a relationship like this. No place for heartache.'

'Do you want me to stay here with you?'

'I'd like to sell the house, too many reminders of Micky, but I want you with me.'

'I want to be with you, I've wanted it all along.'

'And now I believe you. You took a risk telling me.'

'It's all about risk, especially sex, the danger heightens the pleasure.'

'You know, we're all insincere, from Micky to me.'

'But the body does not lie, I've told you how I feel with my hands.'

He made love to her, he took it all away, Micky and the ruined marriage. And Karen knew it was his sexual sincerity that made him gold in bed, she'd known it that first night.